STORIES OF THE

GODS *and*

HEROES

BY SALLY BENSON

ILLUSTRATIONS BY STEELE SAVAGE

DIAL BOOKS FOR YOUNG READERS

NEW YORK

PUBLISHED BY
DIAL BOOKS FOR YOUNG READERS
2 PARK AVENUE
NEW YORK, NEW YORK 10016
COPYRIGHT © 1940 BY SALLY BENSON
COPYRIGHT © RENEWED 1968 BY SALLY BENSON
ALL RIGHTS RESERVED. NO PART OF THIS BOOK
MAY BE REPRODUCED OR TRANSMITTED IN ANY FORM
OR BY ANY MEANS, ELECTRONIC OR MECHANICAL,
INCLUDING PHOTOCOPYING, RECORDING OR BY
ANY INFORMATION STORAGE AND RETRIEVAL SYSTEM,
WITHOUT THE WRITTEN PERMISSION
OF THE PUBLISHER, EXCEPT WHERE PERMITTED BY LAW.
MANUFACTURED IN THE UNITED STATES OF AMERICA. DESIGNED BY PETER DOBLIN.
ISBN 0-8037-8291-8
COBE
24 26 28 30 29 27 25

This book is for
TOBY WHERRY

Contents

Illustrations

Author's Note

THE stories in this book have been taken from *The Age of Fable* by Thomas Bulfinch. I have rewritten some of them entirely, and have cut, edited and clarified others. The dialogue is in most cases the dialogue used by Mr. Bulfinch which he carefully translated from Greek and Latin legends, or from Vergil and Homer. As stories of mythology are not simple, I have made no effort to write them simply, and have followed Mr. Bulfinch's grand, flowing style. Many of the stories used in *The Age of Fable* are not in this book. I found some of them dull, and some of them too involved. The tales of the Trojan War are considerably shortened, and I have left out the adventures of Aeneas altogether. You can find them very well told in many books.

If you are interested in knowing more of mythology, I would suggest that you read *The Age of Fable*. It is the work of a man who conscientiously explored every source to be able to put into one volume myths that have been handed down by people to whom myth was reality.

These stories are not mine. They belong to two races who lived and died, and to Thomas Bulfinch who brought them to life again almost fifty years ago.

Concerning the Pronunciation
of Difficult Names

THE editors themselves have experienced difficulty in pronouncing many of the ancient Greek and Roman names. Therefore, to aid the reader as well as themselves, they have given the proper pronunciation of each of the difficult names where it occurs in the text.

The proper pronunciation appears in parenthesis after the first mention of a particular given name.

CHAPTER I

The Beginning of the World:

A LONG time ago, more years than anyone can count, there was no earth, no sky, sun, moon or stars. There was only space. And, in this space, a huge, shapeless mass hung suspended. It was without color, and it was neither hard nor soft. There was no water on it and no land, not even a blade of grass or the tiniest of living things.

No one knows how long this mass hung, motionless and barren, in the vastness of time. It might have stayed there forever—and there would have been no world for us to live in—had it not been for an invisible force that existed in the midst of the chaos. The force was Nature, who discovered that millions of seeds lay hidden in the hot, thick bulk. Years passed while Nature, appalled by the dreadful waste, wondered how she could give life to still form. She finally appealed to a god who was so far away that he was scarcely aware of the tremendous mass which seemed no more than a tiny speck to him. He listened to Nature and agreed to help her, and with a word, he separated the earth from the sea and the heavens from both. There was a deafening clap of thunder as he spoke the word. Flames leapt high in the air and formed the skies. Beneath them, the air arose, while the earth, being the heaviest, sank to the bottom. The seas boiled and swirled around it, and enormous hot waves, higher than mountains, washed over it. The air would not settle and the din it made as it rushed madly about was deafening. The heavens were jet black, shot with streaks of fire. Only the earth lay quiet, barren and dead.

Nature, realizing that the god had not finished his task and that the seas and skies should be tamed, if life were to exist, pled with another, lesser god to help her once more. They took some of the water from the wild, raging seas, and made calm, peaceful rivers. They raised the earth in places and made mountains. Lakes and valleys formed in the hollows. They smoothed the earth's surface for fertile fields. And they left stony plains for sheep to wander and graze. They scattered seeds, and forests grew to shelter the birds, deer, rabbits and all small timid things.

As the earth and heavens met, there sprang into being a race of gigantic gods called Titans. They had as their ruler a god named Saturn who had many children. Man had not yet been created, so not much is known of Saturn and his reign. Most people believe that he was a cruel and savage monster who devoured his own children. One of his children, Jupiter, escaped this cruel fate and, wishing to overthrow his father, conspired with Prudence, his sister. She mixed a drinking potion which she gave to Saturn, who threw up all the children he had swallowed. Then Jupiter with his brothers and sisters rebelled against Saturn and vanquished him. They sentenced him to Tartarus, one of the regions of Hades, a dreadful place surrounded by three impenetrable walls and the burning waters of the river Phlegethon (fleg'-a-thon). Saturn's brother, Atlas, was forced to bear the heavens on his shoulders for eternity.

Jupiter and his favorite brothers, Neptune and Pluto, divided the world in three parts. Neptune said he would rule the ocean, while Pluto, who was a rather melancholy god, chose the Kingdom of the Dead. The earth was to belong to all the gods and Jupiter was chosen to reign over all living creatures: gods, men and beasts.

He chose as his kingdom the very top of a mountain in Thessaly and called it Olympus. Here, with the exception of Neptune and Pluto, all the gods lived. They got along together as most families do, sometimes quarreling and bickering among themselves and, at other times, dwelling amicably together. They were shut off from the earth by a gate of clouds which was guarded by the goddesses known as the Seasons. Each god had a palace of his own, but they all assembled daily in a mammoth hall in Jupiter's abode where they talked over the affairs of the day. They dined on nectar and ambrosia, drink and food so delicious that it cannot be compared with anything in the world, and so miraculous that the tiniest sip or bite would cause the lowliest of men to become immortal. The lovely goddess, Hebe (hee'-bee), served them their food and drink, and Apollo played soft tunes on his lyre, while the Muses sang to his accompaniment.

Apollo, son of Jupiter, was the god of the sun, god of archery and prophecy. Every day he drove his flaming chariot across the skies, bringing the day. His sister, Diana, pale and beautiful, was goddess of the moon.

All the Immortals had kingdoms over which they

ruled. There was Venus, goddess of love and beauty, who sprang from the foam of the sea. As she was born, a soft breeze carried her along the waves to the Isle of Cyprus. Here she was dressed in flowing robes by the Seasons and led to the palace of Jupiter. She wore an enchanted sash, embroidered in glowing colors, which had the power of inspiring love in all who beheld her. As she bowed before Jupiter, all the gods were enchanted by her beauty, and each one asked to have her for his wife. Jupiter finally gave her to Vulcan as a reward for the service he had rendered in forging thunderbolts.

Vulcan was an artist, the son of Jupiter and Juno. He had been born lame and because of this handicap had learned the art of working in metals. He was architect, smith, armorer and chariot builder for the gods, building them houses of shining brass and designing golden shoes that enabled them to walk on water or air and move from place to place with the speed of the wind. He shod the steeds which whirled the celestial chariots through the air, and, most miraculous of all, he endowed the chairs and tables of his design with self-motion so that they could move themselves in and out of rooms. There is a story that his lameness was caused as the result of a quarrel with Jupiter who, incensed at Vulcan for taking Juno's part in a dispute, flung him from the heavens. He was a whole day falling, and he landed on the Island of Lemnos, which was afterwards sacred to him.

Juno, Jupiter's wife, was something of a scold. She was tall and regal-looking, and at times she was apt to interfere in things. Iris, the goddess of the rainbow, was her personal attendant and messenger. The peacock was her favorite bird, because of his pride and splendor.

Cupid, who was small and mischievous, was the god of love and the son of Venus. He loved his mother dearly and accompanied her wherever she went. With his bows and arrows, he shot darts into the hearts of both men and gods, causing them to fall in love with the first person they saw. He never grew up, always remaining a child, probably because his mother wanted him that way.

Minerva, the goddess of wisdom, had no mother. She sprang forth from Jupiter's head, fully armed. She was wise and kind and chose the owl for her favorite bird, deceived by his sage, thoughtful expression. It was one of her tasks to weave the cloth for all the robes worn by the goddesses, and day after day she sat in the shade of the olive trees weaving soft and colorful materials, assisted in her work by the Graces—Euphrosyne (you-froz′-ih-nee), Aglaia and Thalia. The Graces were frivolous, pretty girls who enjoyed presiding over banquets and other social gatherings. They were very elegant, and considered good manners and social arts extremely important.

Mercury, tall, lean and fleet of foot was the god of all gymnastic sports, commerce and even thieving; in fact, he presided over everything that required skill and dexterity. He was Jupiter's messenger and wore a winged cap and winged shoes. In his hand he carried a rod entwined with two serpents. He is said to have invented the lyre. Roaming about the earth one day, he had found a tortoise. He stripped it of its covering and made holes in the shell through which he drew cords of linen, nine of them, in honor of the Muses. He gave the lyre to Apollo and received the rod, which was called the caduceus, from him in exchange.

Bacchus was the god of wine. He was a peaceful, jovial god, famed as a lawgiver and a promoter of civilization, and he liked nothing better than to sit around in the great hall of the palace, eating, drinking and talking.

The Muses were the daughters of Jupiter and Mnemosyne (ne-moz'-ih-nee), who was also known as Memory. Each one had chosen one of the arts as her particular province; Calliope (kah-lie'-o-pee) was the muse of epic poetry, Clio of history, Euterpe (uh-tur'-pah) chose lyric poetry, Melpomene (mel-pom'-eh-nee) liked tragedy, graceful Terpsichore (turp-sik'-uh-ree) loved choral dances and song, sentimental Erato preferred love poetry, studious Urania selected astronomy, while frivolous Thalia enjoyed comedy. They all presided over song and prompted the memory in honor of their mother.

There were the Fates, who spun the thread of human destiny. They carried scissors with which they cut it off when they pleased. Their names were Clotho, Lachesis (lack'-eh-sis) and Atropos. Alecto, Tisiphone (tih-sif'-uh-nee), and Megaera (meh-jee'-ra) were the Furies, who punished secretly. If a criminal escaped the law, or even won acquittal in the courts for his sin, they stung him through his life. They were men's conscience. Nemesis, too, was an avenging goddess who represented the anger of the gods against the proud and insolent.

There were a great many lesser gods and goddesses; Pan, the god of flocks and shepherds, dwelt in Arcadia, a mountainous region where contentment reigned. The Satyrs (sat'-urs) were deities of the woods and fields. They were covered with bristly hair, horns grew on their heads and they had feet like goats'. Then there was Momus, a grotesque fellow, who was god of laughter, and Plutus, cold and grasping, who was god of wealth. The Lars and Penates (peh-nay'-teez) were household gods, the Penates attending to the welfare and prosperity of the family, while the Lars were supposed to be the deified spirits of mortals. They were really kindly ghosts who watched over their descendants.

Janus was the porter of heaven. He opened the year and the first month, January, was named after him. As guardian of the gates, he had two heads so that he could look both ways, back into the past and ahead into the future.

Vesta was a motherly goddess, who presided over the hearth. In her temple, a sacred fire, tended by six priestesses called Vestals, flamed constantly. If the Vestals allowed it to go out, they were severely punished, and the fire was rekindled from the rays of the sun.

The beginning of the world was a time of great peace and happiness. All over the land seeds swelled and burst, and animals came into being. Horses roamed the plains, chipmunks and squirrels played in the trees, deer ran through the woods without fear, and the cats lay in the sun all day and padded softly through the wet grass at night. Fish appeared in the seas and rivers, and the birds were busy building nests. Only the dog was unhappy, because there was no one on earth for him to love.

Now at this time, there lived a god named Prometheus (pro-mee'-thuse), who was one of the Titans. He had escaped punishment at the hands of Jupiter. He was a gigantic creature who could step across rivers as easily as men can step across brooks, and, in two strides, he could reach the top of the highest mountain. Prometheus and his brother, Epimetheus (ep-ih-mee'-thuse), had been selected to guard the animals as they came to life. And Epimetheus decided that he would give each animal a gift that would help it survive in the new wilderness. He gave wings to the birds, claws to the tiger, shells to the turtles, and to the others he gave courage, strength, speed and keenness of mind. Prometheus had promised his brother that he would approve these gifts after they were given, but, in the meantime, he had been thinking that there was need for a nobler animal than any which had sprung from the seeds that lay in the earth and the sea.

One day, as he was resting on the shore, he scooped up a handful of earth and, to amuse himself, began to form an image in the shape of the gods. He moistened it with water from the ocean so that it would hold together, and he modeled the figure standing upright, its face uplifted gazing at the heavens. In the handful of earth, he found a seed; it was different from any seed he had ever seen, larger and more shining. He washed it off in the sea and placed it in the exact center of the statue he had made. The sun beat down on the image, heating it, and a fresh breeze sprang from the sea, cooling it. Like a piece of pottery, it hardened and dried, and, inside, the seed grew and gave it life. The color of the earth faded from it, and it took on the reflections of all around it; blue from the ocean for the eyes, gold from the skies for the hair, the color of the pale sand for the skin, and deep red from the sunset for the lips. Prometheus called it Man.

Taking Man by the hand, Prometheus led him to his brother, Epimetheus, and asked him to bestow a gift, finer and more valuable than any other. Epimetheus hung his head in shame. The last gift, he said, was gone; he had given the giraffe a long neck so it could reach fruit from the tallest trees. While Man waited, naked and unarmed, Prometheus and his brother talked over what they should do. They finally decided to ask Minerva, goddess of wisdom, to help them. It was quite some time before they found her, but they finally came upon her seated at her loom, weaving robes for the goddesses, in the heart of an olive grove.

Hearing their problem, she agreed to accompany

Prometheus to heaven where he might find something belonging to the gods which he could give to Man. They rode up into the sky and as they passed the chariot of Apollo, Prometheus dipped his torch into the sun, and, turning, descended quickly to earth. He handed the torch to Man and gave him fire, the most valuable gift of all. With it, men became the rulers of the world. They heated metals and formed weapons to protect themselves; they made tools to cultivate the fields; they built fires to heat their dwelling places.

When the gods learned that Prometheus, a Titan, had stolen the fire from heaven, they became enraged. He had, they said, made the race of man too powerful by giving him this divine gift. Jupiter, hearing what Prometheus had done, ordered him chained to a rock on Mount Caucasus (kaw'-kah-sus), face upward in the burning sun, where he lay while a vulture gnawed at his liver, which was renewed every time it was eaten.

Now, Prometheus knew a deadly secret which, if he told it, would cause the downfall of Jupiter's throne. What this secret was, no one today knows. For a moment, he thought he would reveal it to save himself, but, immediately, he acknowledged to himself that he had, indeed, stolen the fire from the gods. He accepted his punishment, scorning to tell the secret and comforting himself with the thought that he had given a divine gift: he sacrificed himself to Man whom he had created.

That night, Man slept in a cave. Close to him huddled a dog, growling and twitching in his sleep, while in front of the fire which crackled and leapt in the hollow of a rock, a cat lay purring.

CHAPTER II

Pandora, the First Woman:

ALTHOUGH Jupiter had punished Prometheus for stealing the divine fire from the chariot of the sun, he was not satisfied. He felt the gods should seek retaliation against Man for accepting the stolen gift. Summoning all the gods to the great hall, he asked them what they thought would plague and torment Man the most. It was decided, after many suggestions and arguments, that a woman might harry him and plant seeds of ambition and dissatisfaction in his breast. So, in much the same way as Prometheus had made Man, they brought clay from the earth and created a woman whom they named Pandora.

When she was given life, she was endowed by the gods with every gift; Venus bestowed beauty on her, Mercury gave her the art of persuasion, Apollo donated the love of music, and the Graces trained her in the social arts. Then, Vulcan fashioned an exquisite box of pure gold into which were put all the evils that have plagued mankind ever since—disease, famine, pestilence, fever, envy, greediness, gluttony, hatred and intolerance. It did not seem possible that a thing as lovely as the golden box could contain so many ills.

As they were about to close the box, the gods and goddesses regretted their hasty decision. And, although they were too proud to abandon the idea altogether, they added one beautiful gift that would lessen the pain caused by all the other disasters. This gift was called hope. The gods tucked it down into the bottom and cautioned Pandora not to open the box which was intended as an offering to the man who took her in marriage.

Then, bidding her goodbye, they gave her to Mercury, Jupiter's messenger, who bore her away with him to the earth. Mercury left her with Epimetheus, who was so struck by her unusual beauty and grace that he gladly took her into his home.

Seeing the golden box under her arm, he asked her what it contained, and she answered that she did not know, exactly, but that she had been told to give it to the man she married. She placed it on a table and its brilliance lighted the entire room. Leaving Pandora alone, after cautioning her not to look at the contents of the chest until he asked the advice of his brother, Epimetheus traveled a whole day until he reached Mount Caucasus where Prometheus lay in chains. He related to him all that had happened, and Prometheus, suspecting a trick, told Epimetheus to hasten back and hide the box in a place so remote that no one could ever find it.

In the meantime, Pandora explored her new home. She picked flowers and scattered their petals which were soft and fragrant under foot; she brought cold, sparkling water from the brook that roared over clean stones at the foot of the hill; she took honey from the bees and fruit from the trees. Each time she entered the house, the shining box caught her eye, and, more than once, she stopped to touch it, shake it, and wonder what it might hold. All day long she kept busy, until, as night drew near, she could find nothing else to do. Drawing a chair up to the table on which the box lay, she sat down, hypnotized by its beauty and glitter. Occasionally, she went to the door and looked in the distance to see if either Epimetheus or Man were approaching.

Finally, she took the box from the table and held it, turning it over and over, admiring its exquisite design. It was almost dark and she was all alone.

"Surely," she thought, "it can do no harm to open this lovely thing a mere crack and see what it contains. Is it a crown? A precious jewel? A magic cloak? A gift from the gods must be something both beautiful and rare."

The Furies who were hovering about robed in invisibility, read her thoughts and stung her conscience with tiny pricks. She fumbled with the clasp on the box and loosened it. "Perhaps," she said to herself, "it is a robe of purest gold thread, embroidered with diamonds, rubies and sapphires. And if it is, it would be better if I opened the cask and wore the robe so that I will look more beautiful in Man's eyes."

As she thought this, the Furies stung her madly, but her curiosity was so great that she scarcely felt them. She opened the box a little, and peering in, saw nothing. Angry and emboldened, she opened it wider and saw what at first looked to be a brown, ugly cloud. The cloud moved and separated, and then, with a loud buzzing sound, hundreds of things resembling small insects escaped into the room. Terrified, she tried to close the box, but her hands shook and she could not manage the catch. It was almost empty when she finally slammed the lid, and only one thing remained. This was hope which had lain on the bottom.

She hurriedly placed the box on the table again and ran to the door to see if Epimetheus or Man were in sight. She looked around the room to make sure that none of the evils remained to be seen. She shook her robe in fear that some might lurk in its folds and she combed her hair free of them. Then, she set the table for supper, selecting the ripest fruits, the most delicious berries and the loveliest scented flowers. Pulling her chair far away from the table, she sat down to await Epimetheus and Man.

When they returned, they found her innocently

busy mending their clothes. And she looked so beautiful sitting there, that Epimetheus almost forgot to ask her whether or not she had looked in the box. When he asked her, she pretended for a moment to have no idea what he meant. "The box?" she queried. "Oh, *that* one! It had slipped my mind entirely. Yes, I did open it a little, and there is a lovely, iridescent thing lying in it. It is more beautiful than the rarest jewel, and it is called hope."

"We will keep it there," Epimetheus told her.

She made no mention of the ugly, brown cloud composed of hundreds of ills that had flown out into the world, and it was some time before Epimetheus and Man knew that the box had contained anything but hope. When they did learn, Pandora had so endeared herself to them that they could not punish her. They looked at her sadly, unable to speak. Seeing the disapproval in their eyes, she tried to defend her disobedience. "It is true that I opened the box," she argued. "But it is also true that I allowed the evils to escape into the world. I brushed them from the room. They are not here and cannot harm us. And our house harbors only hope."

34

CHAPTER III

The Flood:

THE first age of man was called the Golden Age. It was an age of innocence and happiness, as the evils which had escaped from Pandora's box had not grown large enough to cause any serious damage. There were no seasons, and perpetual spring reigned. Flowers sprang up without seed, rivers flowed with milk and delicious wine, and even the oak trees yielded golden honey. All things that man needed to sustain him grew in the fields and it was not necessary to sow or reap crops. The forests were majestic, towering to the skies. Few people lived in houses, as the air was so soft and warm, and men lived in the open or roamed from place to place, carefree and content.

After a time, Jupiter decided to shorten the time of spring and divide the year into seasons. Then, houses became necessary to protect the young and aged from the cold. And with the coming of winter and its hardships, flowers drooped on their stems, bitten by frost, and the crops grew brown in the fields. Men learned to plow and cultivate their lands and to rob the forest of its trees to build homes. This was called the Silver Age.

With food growing scarcer, men became more grasping. They clung tightly to the lands they had cultivated and guarded their homes. They became suspicious of their neighbors who had more than they, and tempers flared. They began to quarrel amongst themselves and often blows were exchanged. This was known as the Bronze Age.

Then followed the Iron Age, a period of horror for the inhabitants of the earth. Crime burst on the world and honor fled. Men outwitted their friends and duped them for gain. They built fences around their properties and were proud of their wealth and prestige in the community. They despoiled the forests of wood to build boats, and they sailed out on the sea and robbed it of its treasures. Not satisfied with what the earth produced on its surface, they dug into it and mined ore and metals. They found iron and gold and fashioned them into weapons. And with the weapons, they killed their enemies and wars became common. The earth was red with blood, and the dead and dying lay everywhere, deserted by those they had once called friends. Children even wished their fathers would die so that they could inherit wealth they had not worked for, and family love vanished from the hearts of men.

The gods, appalled by this state of affairs, abandoned the earth, one by one, until only Astraea (ass-tray'-eh), whose name means "Crown of Stars," was left. She was the goddess of innocence and purity, and she stayed on, praying that man would come to his senses and stop the useless slaughter that went on everywhere. Her prayers went unheeded and after a time she took her departure. Sad and weeping, she appealed to Jupiter for protection. He placed her lovingly among the stars, where she became the constellation Virgo.

Then Jupiter, burning with rage at the stupidity of Man and furious that the world had become so vile that even Astraea, symbol of innocence and purity, had been driven from it, summoned all the gods to a mighty council. They came from everywhere, taking the road to the palace of heaven. The road is still visible on clear nights, stretching across the dark blue sky. It is called the Milky Way.

Jupiter addressed the assembly in stern, indignant tones. He told them of the frightful conditions that existed on the earth, and ended his speech by announcing that he intended to destroy every person who dwelt on it and create a new race, unlike the first, which would be more worthy of life. Turning, he seized a thunderbolt in his bare hands and was about to hurl it to earth and wipe out all life, when he realized that such a mighty conflagration would even set heaven afire. He changed his plan and announced that he would flood the world. With the help of all the gods, he captured the north wind which scatters the clouds and chained it up. The south wind was sent out to blow the clouds together and soon the sky was pitch black and threatening. There was a terrific clash as the clouds met and rain fell in torrents. Fields were flooded, crops destroyed, and fruit was beaten from the trees. He called on his brother Neptune to loose the rivers from their course, and rout the ocean from its bed. He implored Pluto to rock the land with violent earthquakes. The sea washed over its shores. Cattle, fowl, men and houses were swept away in the torrent, and the temples of the gods, long neglected by man, fell into the waters. The whole world was a mighty

sea. Here and there, for a while, one could see a few men who had taken to their boats or sought protection on a hilltop, but soon these disappeared in the swirl of the angry flood. Animals struggled to swim, and the birds, weary of wing, found no resting place and fell to their death.

Only one mountain rose above the maddened waters and this was called Parnassus. And on this mountain a man and his wife found refuge with some of the innocent creatures of the earth. Their names were Deucalion (du-kay'-lee-un), and Pyrrha, and they were descendants of Prometheus who had allowed himself to be tortured through eternity for the sake of mankind. Deucalion and Pyrrha had taken no part in the warfare and hatred that had swept the earth. He was a just, honest man and she was a faithful worshipper of the gods. Looking down from Olympus, Jupiter saw them clinging to the rocks on Parnassus, the water already washing about their feet and ankles. Remembering the blameless lives they had led, he unchained the north wind to drive away the clouds, and Neptune directed Triton to blow on his shell and sound a retreat to the waters. The sea returned to its bed and the rivers subsided.

Then, Deucalion said to Pyrrha, "O my wife, only

surviving woman, joined to me first by the ties of kindred and marriage and now by a common danger, would that we possessed the power of our ancestor, Prometheus, and could renew the race as he first made it! But as we cannot, let us seek yonder temple and inquire of the gods what remains for us to do."

They walked toward the temple, slipping and falling on rocks covered with slime. It was almost in ruins, and no fire burned on its altars. There they kneeled and prayed to the goddess to help them. The oracle answered, "Depart from the temple with heads veiled and garments unbound, and cast behind you the bones of your mother."

They looked at one another in astonishment. Where could they find the bones of their mother? And, if they found them, how could they desecrate them by casting them to the ground?

Finally, Pyrrha spoke. "We cannot obey," she said firmly. "We dare not profane the remains of our parents."

Leaving the temple, they sought protection in a nearby wood and talked over what they should do. Then Deucalion said, "Either my sagacity deceives me, or the command is one we may obey without impiety. The earth is the parent of all. The stones are her bones. These we may cast behind us, and I think this is what the oracle means. At least, it will do no harm to try."

They veiled their faces, unbound their garments, and, picking up stones, they cast them behind them. The stones, striking the earth, grew soft and began to assume shape. Slowly, they showed a vague resemblance to the human form, as a statue does when it is half-finished by a sculptor. The moisture and slime that covered them became flesh; the stony part became bones; the veins in the rocks became human veins. The stones thrown by Deucalion turned into men, and those cast by Pyrrha grew into women.

Thus, a whole new race was created. It was a hardy race whose very bones contained stone from the earth, a race which owed its existence to the ancestors of the hero who had first made Man.

CHAPTER IV

Apollo and the Arrows of Cupid:

WHEN the flood subsided, the earth was covered with silt from the river beds, and all things grew in abundance. Unfortunately, both good and bad things flourished, and on Mount Parnassus, a horrid Python came to life. Every day he got bigger and bigger until, stretching himself to his full length, he could wrap himself around the mountain. At night, he slithered out of the cave where he lay in hiding and descended to the towns and villages below. He seized innocent children from their beds and, carrying them away to his foul-smelling den, he crunched them up and ate them. Terror reigned throughout the countryside, and mothers stayed awake all night listening for the squirming approach of the horrid reptile. Doors were barred and windows locked, but

the Python was so powerful he could break the strongest lock or smash the heaviest wood.

Finally, Apollo, hearing of the plight of the frightened families, resolved to slay the monster. He armed himself with bows and arrows and journeyed to the cave where the Python slept, drowsy with the blood of his victims. Apollo called him forth and dared him to fight. He showed the beast his bows and arrows, puny weapons used against the timid hare. Enraged by these taunts, the Python dragged his slimy length from the cave, his breath hot, his eyes red with rage.

The battle lasted four hours, until, at last, Apollo aimed an arrow at the serpent's vitals, and killed him.

There was great rejoicing in the land and, to commemorate the slaying of the Python, Apollo organized the Pythian games, in which the victor was crowned with a wreath of beech leaves, the laurel not yet having been adopted by Apollo as his own tree. The Pythian games were next in importance to the Olympic games. They took place near Delphi, in the third year of each Olympiad, and were continued as late as 394 A.D.

One day, shortly after his battle with the Python, Apollo saw Cupid, the son of Venus, playing with his bows and arrows. He stopped to talk to the boy, asking, "What have you to do with warlike weapons, saucy boy? Leave them for hands worthy of them. Behold the conquest I have won by means of them over the vast serpent who stretched his poisonous body over acres of the plain! Be content with your torch, child, and kindle up your flames, as you call them, where you will, but presume not to meddle with my weapons."

Cupid, like all children, resented being reminded that he was only a child, and answered, "Your arrows may strike all things, Apollo, but mine shall strike you."

He clambered up on a rock of Parnassus and drew from his quiver two arrows of different workmanship; one to incite love and the other to repel it. The first was of pure gold with a sharp point; the second was of lead and had a blunt point. With the leaden shaft he struck Daphne, a lovely nymph, daughter of the river god, Peneus (peh-nee'-us). And with the golden arrow, he struck Apollo through the heart. As soon as the arrow touched his heart, Apollo fell in love with Daphne, while she, the leaden shaft piercing her breast, abhorred him.

Daphne was both wild and beautiful. She liked to roam through the woods, giving chase to its untamed creatures, and bathing in the cold, clear brooks that tumbled down the mountains. The thought of marriage was distasteful to her and she cherished her freedom. Apollo, Cupid's arrow in his heart, could not bear to be away from her, and he followed her through the woods, pleading his cause. It was strange that he who gave oracles to the world, was not wise enough to look into his own future. "Stay!" he called. "Stay, lovely daughter of Peneus! I am not a foe. Do not fly from me as a lamb flies from a wolf or a dove the hawk. You make me miserable for fear you should fall and hurt yourself on these stones, and I should be the cause. Pray run slower, and I will follow slower. I am no clown, no rude peasant. Jupiter is my father, and I am lord of Delphos and Tenedos (ten′-eh-duz), and know all things, present and future. I am the god of song and the lyre. My arrows fly true to the mark. But, alas! An arrow more fatal than mine has pierced my heart! I am the god of medicine, and know the virtues of all healing plants! Alas! I suffer a malady that no balm can cure."

Daphne ran to her father and, throwing her arms about his neck, begged him, "Dearest father, grant me this favor, that I may always remain unmarried like Diana."

Her father kissed her tenderly and gave his consent, adding sadly, "Your own face will forbid it."

Comforted, she fled once more to the woods, her garments flowing in the wind and her unbound hair streaming behind her. Sped on by Cupid and growing impatient, Apollo gained on her in the race. They flew fast as the wind, he on wings of love and she on wings of fear. At last, she was almost exhausted and, feeling that she could run no farther, she fell to the ground. "Help me, Peneus!" she called to her father. "Open the earth to enclose me or change my form which has brought me into this danger."

She had no sooner spoken than a stiffness seized her limbs. Her body was softly enclosed in a tender bark; her hair became shining leaves; her arms became branches; her feet stuck fast in the ground, as a root; her face became a treetop, retaining nothing of its former self but its beauty.

Apollo stood amazed. He touched the stem and felt Daphne's flesh tremble under the new bark. He gathered the branches into his arms and kissed the wood. The branches shrank from his lips. "Since you cannot be my wife," he said, "you shall assuredly be my tree. I will wear you for my crown. I will decorate you with my harp and my quiver. And when the great Roman conquerors march triumphantly to the Capitol, you shall be woven into wreaths for their brows. And, as eternal youth is mine, you shall also be always green and your leaf know no decay."

Daphne, now a graceful laurel tree, swayed in the breeze in gratitude.

CHAPTER V

Phaeton, and the Chariot of the Sun:

WHEN the world was still very new, there lived a little boy named Phaeton (fay'-eh-tun) who was the son of Apollo and the nymph Clymene (klim'-eh-nee). He was very proud of his noble birth and boasted about it to his schoolmates. One of them laughed at the idea of an ordinary little boy being the son of a god, and Phaeton, enraged by his companion's doubt, ran to his mother. "If," he said, "I am indeed of heavenly birth, give me, mother, some proof of it."

Clymene stretched her arms toward the skies and swore, "I call to witness the sun which looks down upon us that I have told the truth. If I speak falsely, let this be the last time I behold light. But it needs not much labor to go and inquire for yourself. The land whence the sun rises lies next to ours. Go and demand of him whether he will own you as his son."

Phaeton was wild with delight. His mother prepared him for the journey and he traveled to India which lies directly toward the sunrise. Full of hope, he neared the place where his father began his course each day.

The Palace of the Sun rested on columns of purest gold, set with glittering jewels. The ceilings were made of polished ivory and the doors were of silver. Vulcan had built it for Apollo, and it was the most magnificent thing he had ever made. On the walls the earth, the sea and the skies were represented. In the sea were the nymphs, playing in the waves, riding on the backs of fishes, or lying on rocks drying their soft green hair. The earth was complete in every detail; even the cities, forests and fields were carved out exactly and tinted in glorious colors. Above lay the beautiful heavens, while each door bore the twelve signs of the zodiac, six on each side.

Phaeton climbed the steep ascent to the palace and entered the hall. He approached his father but was forced to stop, for the light was more than he could bear. Apollo, clad in royal purple robes, sat on a throne encrusted with diamonds. On either side of him stood the Day, the Month, the Year, and, at regular intervals, the Hours. Spring was crowned with a garland of flowers. Summer stood with garments cast aside, a wreath made of spears of ripe grain around her neck. Autumn's feet were stained with the juice of purple grapes. And Winter stood stiff and icy, his hair thick with frost.

Apollo, seeing that the boy was dazzled by the splendor before him, asked him why he had journeyed so far from home.

Phaeton replied, "O, light of the boundless world, Apollo, my father—if you permit me to use that name, give me some proof, I beseech you, by which I may be known as yours."

His father, laying aside the beams that shone all around his head, bade him approach. Then, embracing the boy, he said, "My son, you deserve not to be disowned, and I gladly confirm what your mother has told you. To put an end to your doubts, ask what you will, the gift shall be yours. I call to witness that dreadful lake, which I never saw but which we gods swear by in our most solemn engagements."

It did not take Phaeton long to think of what he wanted. "Let me for one day, my father," he begged, "drive the chariot of the sun across the sky."

Apollo, aghast at the boy's request, repented his promise. He shook his head four times in warning. "I have spoken rashly," he said. "This request I would fain deny. I beg you to withdraw it. It is not a safe boon, nor one, my Phaeton, suited to your youth and strength. Your lot is mortal, and you ask what is beyond a mortal's power. In your ignorance you aspire to do that which not even the gods themselves may do. None but myself may drive the flaming car of day. Not even Jupiter, whose terrible right arm heaves the thunderbolts."

Drawing the boy to him, he went on, "The first part of the way is steep, and such as the horses fresh in the morning can hardly climb. The middle is high up in the heavens, whence I, myself, can scarcely look down and behold the sea and earth stretched beneath me without alarm. The last part of the road descends rapidly, and requires most careful driving. Tethys (teeth'-is), mother of the chief rivers of the earth, who is waiting to receive me, often trembles for me lest I should fall headlong. Add to all this, the heaven is all the time turning around and carrying the stars with it. I have to be perpetually on my guard lest that movement, which sweeps everything along, should hurry me away also.

Suppose I should lend you the chariot, what would you do? Could you keep your course while the sphere was revolving under you? Perhaps you think that there are forests and cities, the abodes of the gods, and palaces and temples on the way. On the contrary, the road is through the midst of frightful monsters. You pass by the horns of the Bull, in front of the Archer, and near the Lion's jaws, and where the Scorpion stretches its arms in one direction and the Crab in another.

"Nor will you," he said in warning, "find it easy to guide those horses, with their lungs full of fire that they breathe forth from their mouths and nostrils. I can scarcely govern them myself when they are unruly and resist the reins. Beware, my son, lest I be the donor of a fatal gift. Recall your request while yet you may. Do you ask me for proof that you are sprung from my blood? I give my proof in my fears for you. Look at my face. I would that you could look in my heart. You would see all a father's anxiety.

"Finally," he continued, "look around the world and choose whatever you will of what earth and sea contain. Ask it and fear no refusal. This only I pray you not to urge. It is not honor, but destruction you seek. Why do you hang around my neck and still entreat me? You shall have it if you wish, the oath is sworn and must be kept, but I beg you to choose more wisely."

Apollo looked long and tenderly into his son's eyes, and saw that it was useless to plead with him. Taking him by the hand, he led him to the lofty chariot. It was of gold, the gift of Vulcan. Even the axle was gold, the poles and wheels of gold, while the spokes were made of shining silver. Along the seat, were rows of chrysolites and diamonds, which reflected the brightness of the sun. Phaeton, proud and daring, gazed on the chariot with admiration. As he stood there, early Dawn threw open the purple doors of the east, and a pathway lay before him strewn with roses. The stars moved slowly away, marshalled by the Daystar. Apollo, when he saw the earth beginning to glow and the Moon fade, ordered the Hours to harness up the horses. They led the magnificent steeds forth from the stable full fed with ambrosia, and they attached the reins. Then Apollo bathed his son's face with a powerful oil to protect him from the brightness of the flame. He set the rays on his head and with a sigh filled with foreboding, said, "If, my son, you will in this, at least, heed my advice, spare the whip and hold tight to the reins. The horses go fast enough of their own accord. The labor is to hold them in. You are not to take the straight road directly between the five circles, but turn off to the left. Keep within the limit of the middle zone, and avoid the northern and the southern alike. You will see the marks of the wheels, and they will serve to guide you. And, that the skies and the earth may each receive their due share of heat, go not too high or you will burn the heavenly dwellings, nor too low or you will set the earth on fire. The middle course is safest and best. And now I leave you to your chance, which I hope will plan better for you than you have done for yourself. Night is passing out of the western gates, and we can delay no longer. Take the reins. But, if at last your heart fails you, and you will benefit by my advice, stay where you are in safety and suffer me to light and warm the earth."

Phaeton sprang lightly into the chariot, stood erect, and grasped the reins. He laughingly shouted thanks to Apollo who stood by sadly. The horses snorted impatiently and stamped their feet. The bars were let down and the boundless plain of the universe lay before him. The horses sprang forward, cleaving

the dense clouds, and they outran the morning breezes. It was not long before the steeds realized that the load they carried was lighter than usual, and as a ship without ballast is tossed about on the sea, so the chariot, without its accustomed weight, was dashed about as if empty. They rushed headlong and soon left the traveled road. Phaeton became alarmed and tugged at the reins. But his arms were not strong enough to pull in the maddened horses. Past the Great Bear and Little Bear they sped, scorching them so badly that they would have plunged into the water if that had been possible. The Serpent which lay coiled around the North Pole, torpid and harmless, grew warm and with the heat felt its rage revive.

Phaeton looked down at the earth and he grew pale and his knees shook with terror. He wished that he had never touched his father's horses, never learned his parentage, never begged to drive the chariot. He wanted to kneel and pray, but he did not dare loose the reins. He looked vainly around, back to the goal where he began his mad ride, and ahead to the realms of the sunset. They seemed very far away. In his fright, he forgot the names of the horses. He saw the Scorpion extending his two great arms, his tail and crooked claws stretching over two signs of the Zodiac. His courage failed at the sight of the creature reeking with poison and menacing with his fangs, and the reins fell from his hands.

The horses, when they felt them slack on their backs, dashed off into the unknown regions of the sky, in among the stars, hurling the chariot over pathless places, now high up in heaven, now down almost to the earth. The Moon saw with astonishment her brother's chariot running beneath her own. The clouds began to smoke, and the mountain tops broke into flames. Below, the fields were parched and the plants withered, and the trees were ablaze. The fire spread, and great cities burned. People were trapped in their houses and perished in the flames. Athos, Taurus, Tmolus (tmoh'-lus), and Oeta (ee'-teh), great mountains that had been covered with magnificent trees, were like white hot torches. Ida, once celebrated for lovely fountains, was dried up. The two peaks of Parnassus blazed fiercely, and even Rhodope (rod'-uh-pee) was forced to part with his snowy crown. Scythia, Caucasus, Ossa and Pinus crackled in the heat. The Alps and the Apennines, lost in clouds, smouldered.

Phaeton beheld the whole world on fire. The heat

was intolerable and the air he breathed was like the air of a furnace. Burning ashes filled the skies and the smoke was pitch black. Still the chariot dashed on. The people of Aethiopia became black because of the blood being forced so suddenly to the surface of their skins, and the Libyan desert was dried up to the condition in which it remains to this day. The Nymphs of the fountains, with disheveled hair, mourned their waters, and the rivers boiled in their beds. Tanais smoked, and Caicus, Xanthus (zanth'us), and Meander. Babylonian Euphrates, the Ganges (gan'-jeez), Tagus (tay'gus), with its golden sands, and Cayster where the swans glide, bubbled and seethed. The Nile fled and hid its head in the desert, and there it still hides. The earth cracked open, and through the chinks, light broke into Tartarus and frightened the king and queen of the shadows. The sea shrank up, and where there had once been water was now a dry plain, and the mountains that lay beneath the waves lifted their heads and became islands. The fishes sought the lowest depths, and the dolphins no longer ventured to sport on the surface. Even Nereus (near'-use) and his wife, Doris, with the Nereids (near'-ee-ids), their daughters, sought the deepest caves for safety. Three times,

Neptune tried to raise his head above the water and three times he was driven back by the heat. The earth, surrounded by the boiling waters, with her head and shoulders bare, screened her face with her hand, looked up to heaven, and with a voice parched with the heat, called upon Jupiter. "O ruler of the gods," she cried, "if I have deserved this treatment, and it is your will that I perish with fire, why withhold your thunderbolts? Let me at least fall by your hand. Is this the reward of my fertility, of my obedient service? Is it for this that I have supplied herbage for cattle, and fruits for men, and frankincense for your altars? But if I am unworthy of regard, what has my brother Ocean done to deserve such a fate? If neither of us can incite your pity, think, I pray you, of your own heaven, and behold how both the poles are smoking which sustain your palace, which must fall if they be destroyed. Atlas faints, and scarce holds up his burden. If sea, earth and heaven perish, we fall into ancient Chaos. Save what yet remains to us from the devouring flame. O, take thought for our deliverance in this awful moment!"

Overcome with heat and thirst, earth could say no more. Jupiter, calling to witness all the gods, including Apollo who had lent the chariot, and show-

ing them that all was lost unless something was done immediately, mounted the high tower from which he sends the clouds abroad and hurls the forked lightnings. Looking about, he could not find a single cloud to interpose for a screen to the earth, nor was there a shower that had not been exhausted. He thundered, and brandishing a lightning bolt in his right hand, launched it against Phaeton and struck him from the seat. Phaeton, with his hair on fire, fell headlong, like a shooting star, and Eridanus, the great river, received him and cooled his burning body.

The earth burned more feebly and soon the fires abated. Apollo caught the reins of the runaway steeds and led them to their stable. Clouds gathered once more and the rain fell to refresh the rivers.

Apollo, sick at heart, mourned the fate of his reckless son. And the Naïades (nay′-ah-deez), lifting his young body from the depths of the river, built a tomb for him, and inscribed these words upon the stone:

Driver of Phoebus' chariot, Phaeton,
Struck by Jove's thunder, rest beneath this stone.
He could not rule his father's car of fire,
Yet was it much so nobly to aspire?

Phaeton's sisters, the Heliades (heh-lie'-a-deez), mourned for their little brother and were turned into poplar trees on the banks of the river. And, as their tears continued to flow, they became amber as they dropped into the stream.

CHAPTER VI

The Golden Touch of King Midas:

THERE was a time when the people of Phrygia had no king. They appealed to the oracle to send them a man to rule over their country, and the oracle answered that the man who would be their sovereign would be of humble birth and arrive in the city in a wagon drawn by oxen. While the people were deliberating over what to do, a poor countryman named Gordius drove to town in his wagon with his wife and his little son, Midas. The crowds, seeing him approach and believing him to be the man destined to rule them, acclaimed him and made him king. He dedicated his wagon to the deity of the oracle and tied it up in its place with a fast knot. This was the celebrated Gordian knot, of which it was said that whoever should untie it should become lord of all

Asia. Many tried to untie it, but none succeeded till Alexander the Great, in his career of conquest, came to Phrygia. He tried his skill with as ill success as the others, and finally, growing impatient, he drew his sword and cut the knot. When he later conquered all Asia, people thought that he had fulfilled the oracle's prophecy.

Gordius ruled over his country wisely and when he died, his son Midas succeeded to the throne. Now, in the neighboring country of Caria, there lived a king named Silenus (sigh-lee'-nus). He had introduced the worship of Bacchus into his kingdom and consequently had been named foster father to the god. He was a very old man and a very merry one, and he liked to give large banquets, sometimes eating and drinking more than was good for him. One day, after a tremendous feast, he wandered away by himself, and was unable to find his way home again. He lay down in a wheat field, where he was found by some peasants who carried him to their king, Midas. Midas recognized him and treated him hospitably, entertaining him for ten days and ten nights with an unceasing round of jollity. On the eleventh day, he brought Silenus back and restored him safely to Bacchus. Bacchus was so grateful that his foster father had been returned to him unharmed that he offered Midas his choice of a reward, whatever he might wish.

As a child, some ants had put grains of wheat into the mouth of Midas which made him prudent and thrifty almost to a fault. He considered wealth the most important thing in the world. When Bacchus asked him what he wished, he requested that whatever he might touch should be changed into gold. Bacchus consented, warning Midas that he had not made a wise choice.

Midas went his way, rejoicing in his newly acquired power, which he hastened to put to the test. He could not believe his eyes when he found that a twig of an oak, which he plucked from the branch, became gold in his hand. He took up a stone; it changed to gold. He touched a piece of sod; it did the same. He took an apple from the tree, and it turned hard and shiny in his hands. His joy knew no bounds, and as soon as he got home he ordered the servants to set a splendid repast on the table. Hungry from his journey, he sat down to eat. But to his dismay, the bread he crumbled changed to gold and broke his teeth when he tried to bite it; the wine in his goblet poured down his throat like molten metal.

In anger he wished to divest himself of the power

he had longed for. He hated the gift he had craved. But all in vain. Starvation seemed to await him. He raised his arms, all shining in gold, in prayer to Bacchus, begging to be delivered from his glittering destruction.

Bacchus felt that the greedy king had learned his lesson and took pity on him. "Go," he said, "to the river Pactolus (pack-tole'-us), trace the stream to its fountainhead. There plunge your head and body in, and wash away your fault and its punishment."

Midas hurriedly prepared himself for the trip, and hungry and weak made his way to the source of the river. Obeying the god's instructions, he plunged his head and body in the waters. He had scarcely touched them before the gold-creating power passed into them, and the river sands changed into gold, as they remain to this day.

Midas returned home a changed man. He hated wealth and splendor and dwelt in the country, worshipping Pan, the god of the fields. Pan, who was a rather boastful fellow, one day dared to compare the music of his piping with that of Apollo, and he challenged the god of the lyre to a trial of skill. Apollo accepted the challenge, and Tmolus, the mountain god, was chosen umpire. He took his seat

and cleared the trees away from his ears to listen.
At a given signal, Pan blew on his pipes, and with his
rustic melody charmed his own ears and those of his
faithful follower, Midas. Then Tmolus turned his
head toward Apollo, and all his trees turned with him.
The sun god arose, his brow wreathed with Parnas-
sian laurel in memory of Daphne, his robe of Ty-
rolean purple sweeping the ground. In his left hand
he held the lyre, and with his right hand struck the
strings.

Enchanted with the harmony, Tmolus at once

awarded the victory to the god of the lyre, and all but Midas acquiesced in the judgment. He made a great fuss and questioned the justice of the award. Apollo announced that he would not suffer such a depraved set of ears to wear the human form any longer, and with a word, he caused them to grow long and hairy, and movable on their roots. In short, to be on the same pattern as the ears of an ass.

Midas was mortified at the change in his appearance and to hide his misfortune, he covered his head with a large turban. His hairdresser knew his secret, but Midas had cautioned him not to mention it, and threatened him with dire punishment if he dared disobey. The hairdresser found it too much for his discretion to keep the hilarious secret. He went out into the meadow, dug a hole in the ground, and, stooping down, whispered the story and covered it up. Before long a thick bed of reeds sprang up in the meadow, and as soon as it had gained its growth began whispering the story. From that day to this, every time a breeze passes over the place, the reeds laughingly tell the story of the ears of King Midas.

CHAPTER VII

The Reward of Baucis and Philemon:

ONCE upon a time, Jupiter assumed human shape and taking his son Mercury journeyed to Phrygia. Mercury had left his wings behind so that no one would know he was a god, and the two presented themselves from door to door as weary travelers, seeking rest and shelter. They found all doors closed to them as it was late, and the inhospitable inhabitants would not bother to let them in. At last, they came to a small thatched cottage where Baucis (bos'-is), a feeble old woman and her husband, Philemon (fih-lee'-mon), lived. They were a kindly couple, not ashamed of their poverty, and when the two strangers knocked at their door, they bade them enter. The old man placed a seat, on which Baucis, bustling and attentive, spread a cloth, and begged his guests to sit down.

Then Baucis raked out the coals from the ashes and kindled up a fire, fed it with leaves and dry bark, and with her scanty breath blew it into flames. She brought split sticks and dry branches out of a corner, broke them up, and placed them under a small kettle. Philemon collected some pot-herbs in the garden, and she shred them from the stalks and prepared them for the pot. He reached down with a forked stick a flitch of bacon hanging in the chimney, cut a small piece, and put it in the pot to boil with the herbs. A beechen bowl was filled with warm water, that their guests might wash. Host and visitors talked amicably together.

On the bench designed for the guests, a cushion stuffed with seaweed was laid; and a cloth, only produced on great occasions, was spread over that. The old lady, with her apron on, set the table with trembling hands. When the table was fixed, she rubbed it down with sweet-smelling herbs, and upon it she set some of chaste Minerva's olives, some cornel berries preserved in vinegar, and added radishes and cheese, with eggs lightly cooked in the ashes. Everything was served in earthenware dishes, and an earthenware pitcher with wooden cups stood beside them. When all was ready, the stew, smoking hot, was set

on the table. Some wine, mild and sweet, was served, and for dessert they offered wild apples and honey. Over and above all, there were the friendly faces and simple, hearty welcome of the old couple.

As the visitors ate and drank, Baucis and Philemon were astonished to see that the wine, as fast as it was poured out, renewed itself in the pitcher. Struck with terror, they recognized their heavenly guests and falling to their knees, implored forgiveness for the poor entertainment. They had an old goose which they kept as the guardian of their humble cottage and they decided to sacrifice him in honor of their illustrious visitors. But the goose was too nimble and eluded the elderly couple, and at last he took shelter between the gods themselves.

Jupiter and Mercury forbade it to be slain, and spoke in these words: "We are gods. This inhospitable village shall pay the penalty of its impiety. You alone shall go free from the chastisement. Quit your house and come with us to the top of yonder hill."

Baucis and Philemon hastened to obey and labored up the steep ascent. They had reached up to an arrow's flight of the top, when they beheld all the country they had left sunk into a lake, only their own house left standing. While they gazed with wonder at the sight, their house was changed into a temple. Columns took the place of the corner-posts, the thatch grew yellow and turned to gold, the floors became marble, the doors were enriched with exquisite carvings and ornaments of gold.

Then Jupiter spoke to them kindly. "Excellent old man, and woman worthy of such a husband," he said, "speak! Tell us your wishes. What favor have you to ask us?"

Philemon whispered to his wife for a few minutes,

and then declared to the gods their united wish. "We ask to be priests and guardians of this your temple. And since we have passed our lives in love and concord, we wish that one and the same hour may take us both from life, that I may not live to see her grave nor be laid in my own by her."

Their prayers were granted. They were keepers of the temple as long as they lived. When they were very old, as they stood one day before the steps of the sacred temple and were telling the story of the place to some visitors, Baucis saw Philemon begin to put forth leaves, and old Philemon saw Baucis changing in a like manner. And now a leafy crown had grown over their heads. As long as they could speak they exchanged parting words. "Farewell, dear spouse," they said together, as the bark closed over their mouths.

Still on a certain hill in Phrygia, stand a linden tree and an oak enclosed by a low wall. Not far from the spot is a marsh, formerly good habitable land, but now dotted with pools, the haunt of fen-birds and cormorants. They are all that is left of the town and of Baucis and Philemon.

CHAPTER VIII

The Underground Palace of Pluto:

WHEN Jupiter and his brother had defeated the Titans and banished them to Tartarus, a new enemy rose up against the gods. They were the giants Typhon, Briareus (bree-ar'-use), Enceladus (en-sell'-ah-duz) and their brothers. Some of them had a hundred arms, and they breathed out flames that scorched everyone who came near them. They were finally conquered and buried alive under Mount Aetna, where they still sometimes struggle to get loose, and shake the whole island with earthquakes. Their breath comes up through the mountain, and is what men call the eruption of the volcano.

The fall of these monsters shook the earth. And Pluto became alarmed and feared that his kingdom would be laid open to the light of day. He mounted to his chariot drawn by jet black horses, and made a tour of inspection to see the extent of the damages. Venus, who was sitting on Mount Eryx (ee'-ricks), playing with her son, Cupid, saw him, and said, "My son, take your darts with which you conquer all, even Jupiter himself, and send one into the breast of yonder dark monarch who rules the realms of Tartarus. Why should he alone escape? Seize the opportunity to extend your empire and mine. Do you not see that even in heaven some despise our power? Minerva, the wise, and Diana, the huntress, defy us. And there is that daughter of Ceres (see'-reez), Proserpina who threatens to follow their example. Now do you, if you have any regard for your own interest or mine, join Proserpina and Pluto in one."

Cupid unbound his quiver and selected his sharpest and truest arrow. Then, straining the bow against his knee, he attached the string, and shot the arrow with its barbed point right into Pluto's heart.

At the moment the arrow struck him, Pluto was driving through the vale of Enna, a lovely spot near a lake surrounded by woods. Here Proserpina, daughter of Ceres, was playing with her companions, gathering lilies and violets and filling her basket and apron with them. Pluto looked down from his chariot and fell in love with her. He ordered his horses to descend to the earth and, snatching Proserpina away from her helpless playmates, he carried her off. She screamed for help, and in her fright she dropped the corners of her apron and let the flowers fall.

Pluto urged his steeds on, calling them each by name and throwing their iron-colored reins loose over their necks. When he reached the River Cyane and it rose in anger to stop his mad flight, he struck the river bank with his trident, and the earth opened and gave him a passage to Tartarus.

Proserpina's companions ran to Ceres and told her that her daughter had been kidnaped. Rushing from the house, the distracted mother set out in search of her little girl. She roamed all over the world, but could find no trace of her. At length, weary and sad, she sat down on a stone, and continued sitting nine days and nine nights in the open air, under the sunlight and moonlight and falling showers. Near the spot where she sat, an old man named Celeus lived. He was out in the field gathering acorns and blackberries and sticks for his fire, when he saw the goddess sitting alone. She had assumed the guise of an old woman. He called to his little girl and told her to ask the old woman if she needed help. The

little girl approached Ceres and said, "Mother"—
and the name was sweet to the forlorn woman's ears
—"why do you sit here alone on the rocks?"

Celeus also stopped, though his load was heavy,
and begged her to come into his cottage, such as it
was.

"Go in peace," Ceres replied. "And be happy in
your daughter. I have lost mine."

As she spoke, tears, or something like tears, for the
gods never weep, fell down her cheeks. The old
man and the child wept with her. Then, he said,
"Come with us, and despise not our humble roof; so
may your daughter be restored to you in safety."

Ceres arose from the stone. "Lead on," she said.
"I cannot resist that appeal."

As they walked Celeus told her that his only son,
a little boy, lay very sick, feverish and sleepless. They
entered the cottage and Metanira, wife of Celeus,
received Ceres kindly, even though she was sad over
the hopeless condition of her child. The goddess
stooped and kissed the lips of the sick boy. Instantly
the paleness left his face and healthy vigor returned
to his body. The whole family was delighted. They
spread the table for a feast, and put upon it curds
and cream, apples and honey in the comb. While

they ate, Ceres took some poppies and squeezed their juice into the child's mug of milk.

When night came and all was still, she arose and, taking the sleeping boy in her arms, she moulded his limbs with her hands and uttered over him three times a solemn charm. Then she laid him in the ashes in the fireplace. His mother, who had been watching, sprang forward with a cry and snatched the child from the fire. Ceres assumed her own form and a divine splendor shone all around. She said sadly, "Mother, you have been cruel in your fondness to your son. I would have made him immortal, but you have frustrated my attempt. Nevertheless, he shall be great and useful. He shall teach men the use of the plough and the rewards which labor can win from the cultivated soil."

So saying she wrapped a cloud about her, and mounting her chariot, rode away.

Throughout the world Ceres searched for her daughter, passing from land to land and across seas and rivers, till at length she returned to Sicily and stood by the banks of the River Cyane, where Pluto had made the passage to his own dominions. The river nymph would have gladly told the goddess all she had witnessed, but she dared not, for fear of

Pluto. So she only ventured to take up the girdle which Proserpina had dropped in her flight and waft it to the feet of the mother. Ceres, seeing the girdle, was no longer in doubt of her loss, but she did not yet know the cause, and laid the blame on the innocent land. "Ungrateful soil," she cried, "which I have endowed with fertility and clothed with herbage and nourishing grain, no more shall you enjoy my favors."

She caused a curse to fall on the land, and the cattle died, the plough broke in the furrow; the seed failed to sprout, and there was too much sun and too much rain. The birds stole the seeds, and thistles and brambles were the only growth. Seeing this desolation, the fountain Arethusa interceded for the land. "Goddess," she said, "blame not the land. It opened unwillingly to yield a passage to your daughter. I can tell you of her fate, for I have seen her. This is not my native country, I came hither from Elis. I was a woodland nymph, and delighted in the chase. They praised my beauty, but I cared nothing for it, and rather boasted of my hunting exploits. One day I was returning from the wood, heated with exercise, when I came to a stream silently flowing, so clear that you might count the pebbles on the bottom.

The willows shaded it, and the grassy bank sloped down the water's edge. I approached. I touched the water with my foot. I stepped in knee-deep, and, not content with that, I laid my garments on the willows and went in. While I sported in the water, I heard an indistinct murmur coming up as out of the depths of the stream, and made haste to escape to the nearest bank. The voice said, 'Why do you fly, Arethusa? I am Alpheus (al-fee'-us), the god of this stream.' "

"I ran. He pursued. He was not swifter than I, but he was stronger and gained on me, as my strength failed. At last, exhausted, I cried for help to Diana, 'Help me, goddess! Help your votary!' The goddess heard and wrapped me suddenly in a thick cloud. The river god looked now this way and now that, and twice came close to me, but could not find me. 'Arethusa, Arethusa,' he cried. O, how I trembled —like a lamb that hears the wolf growling outside the fold. A cold sweat came over me. My hair flowed down in streams. Where my feet stood there was a pool. In short, in less time than it takes to tell it, I became a fountain. But even in this form Alpheus knew me. Diana then cleft the ground, and I, endeavoring to escape him, plunged into the cavern, and through the bowels of the earth came out here in Sicily. While I passed through the lowest parts of the earth, I saw your lovely Proserpina. She was sad, but no longer showed alarm. Her look was such as became a queen—the queen of Erebus (err'-eh-buss). She is the bride of the monarch of the realms of the dead."

When Ceres heard this she stood for a while like one stupefied. Then she turned her chariot toward heaven and presented herself before the throne of Jupiter. She told the story of her bereavement and implored Jupiter to arrange for the return of her daughter. Jupiter consented on one condition, namely, that Proserpina should not have taken any food during her stay in the underworld. Otherwise, the Fates forbade her release.

Mercury was sent, accompanied by Spring, to demand Proserpina of Pluto. They found Proserpina in the vast halls of the underground palace. She was dressed in queenly robes and wore precious jewels. Pluto had been kind to her, and she had learned to love and respect him, while he was delighted with the young, happy girl who brought laughter and gaiety into his dark life. He had given her everything she had asked, and, if it had not been that she longed to see her mother again, she would gladly have stayed with him forever.

One thing, however, had displeased her; she did not like the tasteless meals that satisfied her husband, and longed for the fresh fruits and berries of the earth. One day, she found a pomegranate in her apron pocket. It had grown dry and hard, but she was so hungry that she bit into it and sucked the sweet pulp from a few of the seeds. When Mercury told her of Jupiter's decision, she burst into tears, and confessed that she had, indeed, eaten the meat from the seeds. Pluto, seeing her sad, grieved with her, and he, himself, pled with Jupiter for her release. Jupiter answered that she should spend half the time on earth with her mother and the other half with Pluto. And Ceres, pacified with this arrangement, restored the earth to her favor.

CHAPTER IX

The Love of Cupid and Psyche:

THERE once lived a king and queen who had three daughters. The two elder daughters were beautiful, but the youngest daughter, Psyche, was the loveliest maiden in the whole world. The fame of her beauty was so great that strangers from neighboring countries came in crowds to admire her, paying her the homage which is only due Venus herself. In fact, Venus found her altars deserted, as men turned their devotion to the exquisite young girl. People sang her praises as she walked the streets, and strewed chaplets and flowers before her.

This adulation infuriated Venus. Shaking her silken locks in indignation, she exclaimed, "Am I then to be eclipsed by a mortal girl? In vain did that royal shepherd whose judgment was approved by

Jupiter himself give me the palm of beauty over my illustrious rivals, Minerva and Juno. I will give this Psyche cause to repent of so unlawful a beauty."

She complained to her son, Cupid, and led him to the land where Psyche lived, so that he could see for himself the insults the girl unconsciously heaped upon his mother. "My dear son," said Venus, "punish that beauty. Give thy mother a revenge as sweet as her injuries are great. Infuse into the bosom of that haughty girl a passion for some low, mean, unworthy being, so that she may reap a shame as great as her present joy and triumph."

Now, there were two fountains in Venus's garden, one of sweet waters, the other of bitter. Cupid filled two amber vases, one from each fountain and, suspending them from the top of his quiver, hastened to Psyche's chamber, where she lay asleep. He shed a few drops from the bitter fountain over her lips, though she looked so beautiful in her sleep that he was filled with pity. Then he touched her side with the point of his arrow. At the touch, she awoke and opened her eyes on Cupid, who was so startled by their blue enchantment that he wounded himself with his own arrow. He hovered over her, invisible, and to repair the damage he had done, he poured the water from the sweet fountain over her silken ringlets.

Psyche, thus frowned upon by Venus, derived no benefit from all her charms. All eyes were still cast eagerly upon her and every mouth spoke her praise, but neither king, royal youth, or common man presented himself to demand her hand in marriage. Her two elder sisters were married to royal princes, but Psyche, in her lonely apartment, wept over her beauty, sick of the flattery it aroused, while love was denied her.

Her parents, afraid that they had unwittingly incurred the anger of the gods, consulted the oracle of Apollo, and received this answer: "The girl is destined for the bride of no mortal lover. Her future husband awaits her on the top of the mountain. He is a monster whom neither the gods nor men can resist."

This dreadful decree of the oracle filled all the people with dismay, and her parents abandoned themselves to grief. But Psyche said, "Why, my dear parents, do you now lament me? You should rather have grieved when the people showered undeserved honors upon me and with one voice called me 'Venus.' I now perceive I am a victim to that name.

I submit. Lead me to that rock to which my unhappy fate has destined me."

She dressed herself in gorgeous robes, and her beauty was so dazzling that people turned away as it was more than they could bear. Then, followed by wailing and lamenting crowds, she and her parents ascended the mountain. On the summit, her father and mother left her alone, and returned home in tears.

While Psyche stood on the ridge of the mountain, panting with fear and sobbing aloud, the gentle Zephyrus (zef'-ih-russ) raised her from the earth and bore her with an easy motion into a flowery dale. There she lay down on a grassy bank and fell asleep. She awoke refreshed, and saw near by a pleasant grove of tall and stately trees. She entered it, and discovered a fountain sending forth clear and crystal waters, and near it stood a magnificent palace that was too stupendous to have been the work of mortal hands. Drawn by admiration and wonder, she walked through the huge doors. Inside, golden pillars supported the vaulted roof, and the walls were hung with delightful paintings. She wandered through the empty rooms marveling at what she saw, when suddenly a voice addressed her. "Sovereign lady," it said, "all that you see is yours. We whose voices you hear are your servants and shall obey all your commands with the utmost care and diligence. Retire, therefore, to your chamber and repose on your bed of down, and when you see fit, repair to the bath. Supper awaits you in the adjoining alcove when it pleases you to take your seat there."

Psyche listened with amazement, and, going to her room, she lay down and rested. Then, after a refreshing bath, she went to the alcove, where a table wheeled itself into the room without any visible aid. It was covered with the finest delicacies and the most wonderful wines. There even was music from invisible performers.

She had not yet seen her destined husband. He came only in the hours of darkness and fled before dawn, but his accents were full of love and inspired a like passion in her. She often begged him to stay and let her behold him, but he would not consent. On the contrary, he charged her to make no attempt to see him, for it was his pleasure, for the best of reasons, to remain concealed. "Why should you wish to behold me?" he asked. "Have you any doubt of my love? If you saw me, perhaps you would fear me, perhaps adore me. But all I ask of you is to love me. I would rather have you love me as an equal than adore me as a god."

This reasoning satisfied Psyche for a time and she lived quite happily alone in the huge palace. But at length she thought of her parents who were in ignorance of her fate, and of her sisters with whom she wished to share the delights of her new home. These thoughts preyed on her mind and made her think of her splendid mansion as a prison. When her husband came one night, she told him of her distress, and at last drew from him an unwilling consent that her sisters should be brought to see her.

So, calling Zephyrus, she told him of her husband's command, and he soon brought them across the mountain down to their sister's valley. They embraced her, and Psyche's eyes filled with tears of joy. "Come," she said, "enter my house and refresh yourselves." Taking them by their hands, she led them into her golden palace and committed them to the care of her numerous train of attendant voices, to refresh themselves in her baths and at her table, and to show them all her treasures. The sight of all these splendid things filled her sisters with envy, and they resented the thought that she possessed such splendour which far exceeded anything they owned.

They asked her numberless questions, and begged her to tell them what sort of person her husband was. Psyche replied that he was a beautiful youth who generally spent the daytime in hunting upon the mountains. The sisters, not satisfied with this reply, soon made her confess that she had never seen him. They then proceeded to fill her bosom with dire suspicions. "Call to mind," they said, "the Pythian oracle that declared that you were destined to marry a direful and tremendous monster. The inhabitants of this valley say that your husband is a terrible and monstrous serpent, who nourishes you for a while with dainties that he may by and by devour you. Take our advice. Provide yourself with a lamp and a sharp knife. Put them in concealment so that your husband may not discover them, and when he is sound asleep, slip out of bed, bring forth your lamp and see for yourself whether what they say is true or not. If it is, hesitate not to cut off the monster's head, and thereby recover your liberty."

Psyche resisted these persuasions as well as she could, but they did not fail to have their effect on her mind, and when her sisters were gone, their words and her own curiosity were too strong for her to resist. She prepared her lamp and a sharp knife, and hid them out of sight of her husband. When he had fallen into his first sleep, she silently arose, and uncovering her lamp beheld him. He lay there, the most beautiful and charming of the gods, with his golden ringlets wandering over his snowy neck and crimson cheek. On his shoulders were two dewy wings, whiter than snow, with shining feathers.

As she leaned over with the lamp to have a closer view of his face, a drop of burning oil fell on his shoulder, and made him wince with pain. He opened his eyes and fixed them full upon her. Then, without saying a word, he spread his white wings and flew out of the window. Psyche cried out and tried to follow him, falling from the window to the ground. Cupid, beholding her as she lay in the dust, stopped his flight for an instant and said, "O foolish Psyche! Is it thus you repay my love? After having disobeyed my mother's commands and made you my wife, will you think me a monster and cut off my head? But go. Return to your sisters whose advice you seem to think better than mine. I inflict no other punishment on you than to leave you forever. Love cannot dwell with suspicion."

He soared into the air, leaving poor Psyche prostrate on the ground.

When she recovered some degree of composure, she looked around her. The palace and gardens had vanished, and she found herself in an open field not far from the city where her sisters dwelt. She went to them and told them the whole story of her misfortune, at which, pretending to grieve, they inwardly rejoiced. "For now," they said, "he will perhaps choose one of us." With this idea, without saying a word of her intentions, each of them rose early the next morning and ascended the mountain and, having reached the top, called upon Zephyrus to receive her and bear her to his lord. Then, leaping into space, and not being sustained by Zephyrus, they fell down the precipice and were dashed to pieces.

Psyche, meanwhile, wandered day and night, without food or rest, in search of her husband. One day, seeing a lofty mountain in the distance, she sighed and said to herself, "Perhaps my love, my lord, inhabits there."

On the mountain top was a temple and she no sooner entered it than she saw heaps of corn, some in loose ears and some in sheaves, with mingled ears of barley. Scattered about lay sickles and rakes, and all the instruments of harvest, without order, as if thrown carelessly out of the weary reapers' hands in the sultry hours of the day.

Psyche put an end to this unseemly confusion by separating and sorting everything to its proper place and kind, believing that she ought to neglect none of the gods, but endeavor by her piety to engage them all in her behalf. The holy Ceres, whose temple it was, finding her so religiously employed, spoke to her, "O Psyche, truly worthy of our pity, though I cannot shield you from the frowns of Venus, yet I can teach you how to best allay her displeasure. Go then, and voluntarily surrender yourself to her, and try by modesty and submission to win her for-giveness, and perhaps her favor will restore you to the husband you have lost."

Psyche obeyed the commands of Ceres and jour-neyed to the temple of Venus. Venus received her in a fury of anger. "Most undutiful and faithless of servants," she said, "do you at last remember that you really have a mistress? Or have you come to see your sick husband, yet laid up with the wound given him by his loving wife? You are so ill-favored and disagreeable that the only way you can merit your lover must be by dint of industry and diligence. I will make trial of your housewifery."

She ordered Psyche to be led to the storehouse of her temple, where a great quantity of wheat, barley, millet, beans and lentils, which was used as food for her pigeons, lay scattered about the floors. Then Venus said, "Take and separate all these grains into their proper parcels, and see that you get it done before evening."

Psyche, in consternation over the enormous task, sat stupid and silent. While she sat despairing, Cupid stirred up the little ant, a native of the fields, to take compassion on her. The leader of the ant-hill, fol-lowed by whole hosts of his six-legged subjects, went to work and sorted each grain to its parcel. And when all was done, the ants vanished out of sight.

At twilight, Venus returned from the banquet of the gods, crowned with roses. Seeing the task done, she exclaimed, "This is no work of yours, wicked one, but his, whom to your own and his misfortune you have enticed." So saying, she threw her a piece of black bread for her supper and went away.

Next morning Venus ordered Psyche to be called and said to her, "Behold yonder grove which stretches along the margin of the water. There you will find sheep feeding without a shepherd, with gold-shining fleeces on their backs. Go, fetch me a sample of that precious wool from every one of their fleeces."

Psyche obediently went to the river side, prepared to do her best to execute the command. But the river god inspired the reeds with harmonious murmers, which seemed to say, "O maiden, severely tried, tempt not the dangerous flood, nor venture among formidable rams on the other side, for as long as they are under the influence of the rising sun they burn with a cruel rage to destroy mortals with their sharp horns or rude teeth. But when the noontide sun has driven the cattle to the shade, and the serene spirit of the flood has lulled them to rest, you may then cross in safety, and you will find the woolly gold sticking to the bushes and the trunks of the trees."

She followed the compassionate river god's instructions and soon returned to Venus with her arms full of the golden fleece. Venus, in a rage, cried, "I know very well it is by none of your own doings that you have succeeded in this task. And I am not satisfied yet that you have any capacity to make yourself useful. But I have another task for you. Here, take this box, and go your way to the infernal shade and give this box to Proserpina and say, 'My mistress, Venus, desires you to send her a little of your beauty, for in tending her sick son, she has lost some of her own.' Be not too long on your errand, for I must paint myself with it to appear at the circle of gods and goddesses this evening."

Psyche was now sure that her destruction was at hand, being obliged to go with her own feet down to the deathly regions of Erebus. So as not to delay, she went to the highest tower prepared to hurl herself headlong from it down to the shades below. But a voice from the tower said to her, "Why, poor unlucky girl, dost thou design to put an end to thy days in so dreadful a manner? And what cowardice makes thee sink under this last danger who hast been so miraculously supported in all thy former perils?"

Then the voice told her how she might reach the realms of Pluto by way of a certain cave, and how to avoid the perils of the road, how to pass by Cerberus (sir'-ber-us), the three-headed dog, and prevail on Charon (kay'-ron), the ferryman, to take her across the black river and bring her back again. And the voice added, "When Proserpina has given you the box filled with her beauty, of all things this is chiefly to be observed by you, that you never once open or look into the box, nor allow your curiosity to pry into the treasure of the beauty of the goddesses."

Psyche, encouraged by this advice, obeyed in all things, and traveled to the kingdom of Pluto. She was admitted to the palace of Proserpina, and without accepting the delicate seat or delicious banquet that was offered her, but content with coarse bread for her food, she delivered her message from Venus. Presently the box was returned to her, shut, and filled with the precious commodity. She returned the way she came, happy to see the light of day once more.

Having got so far successfully through her dangerous task, a desire seized her to examine the contents of the box. "What," she said to herself, "shall I, the carrier of this divine beauty, not take the least bit to put on my cheeks to appear to more advantage in the eyes of my beloved husband!" She carefully opened the box, and found nothing there of any beauty at all, but an infernal and truly Stygian sleep, which, being set free from its prison, took possession of her. She fell down in the road, unconscious, without sense or motion.

Cupid had recovered from his wound and was no longer able to bear the absence of his beloved Psyche. He slipped through the smallest crack in the window of his chamber and flew to the spot where Psyche lay. He gathered up the sleep from her body and closed it again in the box. Then he waked Psyche with a light touch from one of his arrows.

"Again," he said, "hast thou almost perished by the same curiosity. But now perform exactly the task imposed on you by my mother, and I will take care of the rest."

Swift as lightning, he left the earth and penetrated the heights of heaven. Here he presented himself before Jupiter with his supplication. The god lent a favoring ear, and pleaded the cause of the lovers so earnestly with Venus that he won her consent. Then he sent Mercury to bring Psyche up to the heavenly assemblage, and when she arrived, he handed her a cup of ambrosia and said, "Drink this, Psyche, and be immortal. Nor shall Cupid ever break away from the knot in which he is tied, but these nuptials shall be perpetual."

Psyche became at last united to Cupid forever.

CHAPTER X

Cadmus and the Serpent:

AGENOR (a-jee′-nor), king of Phoenicia, had two children, a son and a daughter. The daughter, whose name was Europa, was a beautiful maiden, both gentle and kind. One day Jupiter caught a glimpse of her as she wandered in the gardens of her father's palace, and immediately fell in love with her. Determined to possess her, he assumed the disguise of a beautiful white bull and mingled with the flocks that grazed in the fields. Every day when Europa passed by he came near the fence and pawed the ground and shook his head until she took notice of him. Enchanted by his gentleness, she made garlands of flowers which she hung around his neck, and, eventually, she dared climb on his back and ride slowly around the meadow. She soon tired of this tame sport and longed to ride through the countryside on her new mount. She opened the gates and, with a bound, the bull sped through, Europa clinging to his neck. Away and away he dashed until he came to the sea. He plunged in, and swam away with her to the island of Crete.

Her father, finding out that she was gone but unaware of her fate, commanded his son Cadmus to go in search of his sister. Cadmus sought long and far for her, but could not find her. And, not daring to return unsuccessful, he consulted the oracle of Apollo to find out what country he should settle in. The oracle told him that he would find a cow in a field and that he should follow her wherever she might wander, and where she stopped he should build a city and call it Thebes.

Cadmus had hardly left the Castalian cave, from which the oracle was delivered, when he saw a young cow slowly walking before him. He followed her close, offering up prayers to Apollo as he went. The cow went on until she passed the shallow channel of Cephisus (seh-fee′-sus) and came out into the plains of Panope. There she stood still and, raising her broad forehead to the sky, filled the air with her lowings. Cadmus gave thanks and stooped down to kiss the foreign soil. Then, lifting his eyes, he greeted the surrounding mountains. Wishing to offer a sacrifice

to Jupiter, he sent his servants to seek pure water for a libation. Near by stood an ancient grove, which had never been profaned by an ax. And, in the midst of the grove, was a cave covered thickly with undergrowth. Its roof formed a low arch, and on the ground flowed a fountain of purest water. In the cave lurked a horrid serpent, sacred to Mars, god of war. The serpent had a crested head and scales glittering like gold. His eyes shone like fire; his body was swollen with venom; he vibrated a triple tongue, and showed a triple row of teeth. No sooner had the servants dipped their pitchers in the fountain, and the ingushing waters made a sound, than the glittering serpent raised his head out of the cave and uttered a fearful hiss.

The vessels fell from their hands, the blood left their cheeks, and they trembled in every limb. The serpent, twisting his scaly body in a huge coil, raised his head higher than the tallest trees. And while the servants in sheer terror could neither fly from him nor fight, he slew some of them with his fangs, others he squeezed to death, and the rest died from the fumes of his poisonous breath.

Cadmus waited until midday for the return of his men and then went in search of them. He wore a lion's hide and, in addition to his javelin, he carried a lance in his hand. When he entered the wood and saw the lifeless bodies of his men, and the monster with its jaws crimson with blood, he exclaimed, "O faithful friends, I will avenge you or share your death!"

So saying, he lifted a huge stone and threw it with all his force at the serpent. Such a blow would have shaken the wall of a fortress, but it made no impression on the monster. Cadmus next threw his javelin, which penetrated through the serpent's scales and pierced through to his entrails. Fierce with pain, the monster turned his head to see the wound, and attempted to draw out the weapon with his mouth. It broke off and the iron point was left rankling in his flesh. His neck swelled with rage, bloody foam covered his jaws, and the breath from his nostrils poisoned the air. He twisted himself into a circle, then stretched himself out on the ground like the trunk of a fallen tree. As he moved onward, Cadmus retreated before him, holding his spear opposite the monster's open jaws. The serpent snapped at the weapon, and tried to bite its iron point. Cadmus, watching his chance, thrust the spear at a moment when the fierce animal's head was thrown back against the trunk of a tree. The spear entered the serpent's mouth and pinned him to the tree's side. As he struggled in his death, his weight bent the tree almost to the ground.

While Cadmus stood over his vanquished foe, marveling at his vast size, a voice was heard commanding him to take the dragon's teeth and sow them in the earth. He obeyed. He made a furrow in the ground, and planted the teeth. He had scarcely covered them, when the clods began to move and points of spears appeared above the surface of the ground. Next helmets with nodding plumes came up, and next the shoulders, breasts and limbs of men who carried weapons. He had sown a harvest of armed warriors.

Cadmus was alarmed and made ready to fight a new enemy, when one of the men stepped forward and said to him, "Meddle not with our civil war." With that, he smote one of his earth-born brothers with a sword, and he himself fell pierced with an arrow from another. The latter fell a victim to a fourth, until all were slain except five. One of these cast his weapons away and said, "Brothers, let us live in peace!"

These five joined Cadmus in building his city, to

which he gave the name of Thebes. When the city was completed, Cadmus married Harmonia, the daughter of Venus. The gods left Olympus to honor the occasion with their presence, and Vulcan presented the bride with a necklace of surprising brilliancy, his own workmanship. But bad luck hung over the family of Cadmus in consequence of his having killed the serpent, who had been sacred to Mars. Semele and Ino, his daughters, and Actaeon and Pentheus (pen'-thuse), his grandchildren, all perished unhappily. Saddened by their misfortunes, Cadmus and Harmonia left Thebes and migrated to the country of the Enchelians, who received them with honor and made Cadmus their king.

The tragedies of their children still weighed upon their minds, and they resented their exile. One day, homesick and filled with grief, Cadmus said to his wife, "We have been punished all our lives because I slew the monster sacred to Mars. If a serpent's life is so dear to the gods, I would I were myself a serpent!"

No sooner had he uttered these words than he began to change his form. Harmonia in anguish prayed to the gods to let her share his fate. Her prayers were answered, and they both became serpents. To this day they live in the woods; but, re-membering the time when they were human, they have no fear of men, nor do they ever injure any one.

Europa, who was the cause of her unhappy broth-er's wanderings, never saw her father again. She lived happily on the island of Crete and gave birth to three children: Minos, Sarpëdon, and Rhadamanthus (rad-a-man'-thus).

CHAPTER XI

The Magic Ants:

ONE of Europa's children, Minos, became king of Crete, and a war sprang up between the inhabitants of Crete and the people of Athens. Cephalus, who was king of Athens, became alarmed at the turn the battle was taking, and journeyed to the island of Aegina to seek the assistance of his old friend and ally, Aeacus, its king. Cephalus was most kindly received, and was assured of help. "I have people enough," Aeacus (ee'-a-kus) said, "to protect myself and spare you such a force as you need."

"I rejoice to see it," Cephalus replied. "And my wonder has been raised, I confess, to find such a host of youths as I see around me, all apparently of about the same age. Yet there are many individuals whom I previously knew that I look for now in vain. What has become of them?"

Aeacus groaned and said sadly, "I have been intending to tell you and will now do so without more delay, that you may see how from the saddest beginning a happy result sometimes flows."

He asked Cephalus to seat himself in a comfortable chair and ordered some wine that they might drink as they talked. Then he told him the following story: "Those whom you formerly knew," he said, "are dust and ashes. A plague sent by Juno devastated the land. She hated our land because it bore the name of one of Jupiter's favorites. While the disease appeared to spring from natural causes, we resisted it as best we could, by natural remedies. But it soon appeared that the pestilence was too powerful for our efforts, and we yielded. At the beginning, the sky seemed to settle down upon the earth, and thick clouds shut in the heated air. For four months a deadly south wind prevailed. The wells and springs were affected and there was no fresh water to drink. Thousands of snakes crept over the land and shed their poison in the fountains. The lower animals—dogs, sheep, cattle and birds—first succumbed to the disease. The ploughman saw his oxen fall in the midst of their work and lie helpless in the unfinished furrow. The wool fell from the bleating sheep, and they grew thin and died. Horses which had once been foremost in the race, contested the palm no more, but groaned in their stalls and died an inglorious death. The wild boar forgot his rage, and the stag lost his swiftness. The bears no longer attacked the herds.

"Everything languished. Dead bodies lay in the roads, the fields and the woods. The air was poisoned by them. I tell you what is hardly credible, but neither dogs nor birds would touch them, nor would the starving wolves. Next the disease attacked the country people, and then the dwellers in the city. At first the cheek was flushed and the breath drawn with difficulty. The tongue grew rough and swelled, and the dry mouth grew rough and swelled. People gasped for breath. Men could not bear the heat of their clothes or their beds, and lay on the bare ground. And the ground did not cool them. Nor could the physicians help, for the disease attacked them also, and the contact with the sick gave them infections, so that the most faithful were the first victims.

"At last, all hope of relief vanished, and men learned to look on death as the only deliverer from the dread disease. They gave way to every inclination, for nothing mattered to them. All restraint laid aside, they crowded around the wells and the fountains and drank until they died without quenching their thirst. Many had not strength to get away from the water, and died in the midst of the stream which others drank of afterwards. They were so weary of their sickbeds that some would creep forth, and would die on the ground, not strong enough to stand. They seemed to hate their friends, and crawled away from their homes, as if, not knowing the cause of their sickness, they blamed it on the place of their abode. Some were seen tottering along the road, as long as they could stand, while others sank to the earth and turned their dying eyes around to take a last look at what had once been dear to them, before they closed them in death.

"What heart had I left me during all this, or what ought I have had, except to hate life and wish to be with my dead subjects? On all sides my people lay strewn like over-ripened apples beneath the tree, or acorns under the storm-shaken oak. You see yonder a temple on a height? It is sacred to Jupiter. O how many offered prayers there, husbands for wives, fathers for sons! They died in the very act of supplication! How often, while the priest made ready for sacrifice, the victim fell, struck down by disease! At length all reverence for sacred things was lost.

Bodies were thrown out unburied, wood was wanting for funeral piles, men fought with one another for possession of a few sticks. Finally there was none left to mourn. Sons and husbands, old men and youths, perished unlamented.

"Standing before the altar, I raised my eyes to heaven. 'O Jupiter,' I said, 'if thou art indeed my father, and art not ashamed of thy offspring, give me back my people, or take me also away!'

"As I finished speaking, I heard a clap of thunder. 'I accept the omen,' I cried. 'O may it be a sign of a favorable disposition toward me!' There grew by the side of the place where I stood an oak with wide-spreading branches, sacred to Jupiter. I observed a troop of ants busy with their labor, carrying minute grains in their mouths and following one another in a line up the trunk of the tree. Observing their numbers, I said, 'Give me, O father, citizens as numerous as these, and replenish my empty city!'

"The tree shook and there was a rustling sound in its branches, though no wind stirred. I trembled in every limb, yet I kissed the earth and the tree. I would not confess that I hoped, yet I did hope. Night came on and sleep took possession of me. The tree stood before me in my dreams, with its branches all

covered with living, moving creatures. It seemed to
shake and throw down over the ground a multitude
of those industrious, grain-gathering insects. They
appeared to gain in size and grow larger and larger.
By and by, they stood erect, laid aside their super-
fluous legs and their black color. They finally assumed the human form. Then I awoke, and my first
impulse was to chide the gods who had robbed me
of a sweet vision and given me no reality in its place.
Being still in the temple, my attention was caught

by the sound of many voices without, a sound unusual to my ears of late. While I began to think I was still asleep, Telamon, my son, threw open the temple gates and exclaimed, 'Father, approach, and behold things even surpassing your hopes!'

"I went forth. I saw a multitude of men, such as I had seen in my dream, and they were marching in procession in the same manner. While I gazed with wonder and delight, they drew near and, kneeling, hailed me as king. I paid my vows to Jupiter, and allotted the vacant city to the new-born race, and parceled out the fields among them. I called them Myrmidons from the ant, myrmex, from which they sprang. You have seen them. Their dispositions resemble those which they had in their former shape. They are a diligent and industrious race, eager to gain and tenacious of their gains. Among them you may recruit your forces. They will follow you to the wars. They are young in years and bold in heart."

Cephalus, inspired by the miracle, sailed for home with a new army of strong, steady young men who a short while ago had been humble ants.

CHAPTER XII

The Ungrateful Daughter:

MINOS, king of Crete, seeking to enlarge his territories, made war upon Nisus, king of Megara. The siege had lasted six months and the city still held out, as it had been decreed by fate that it could not be taken so long as a certain purple lock of hair remained on King Nisus's head.

Nisus had a daughter named Scylla (sill'-ah). Every day she went to a tower on the city walls which overlooked the plain where Minos and his army were encamped. There she could look down on the tents of the invading army. The siege had lasted so long that she had learned to distinguish the leaders of the forces, and Minos, in particular, excited her admiration. In his plumed helmet with his shield in hand, he was a striking figure, and when he drew his bow, Apollo himself could not have done it more gracefully. But when he laid aside his helmet and rode his white horse, his purple robes flowing in the wind, Scylla was overcome with delight. She envied the weapon that he grasped, the reins that he held. She felt as if she could fly to him through the hostile ranks; she wished she could cast herself down from the tower into the midst of his camp, or open the gates to him—if only she could speak with him.

As she sat in the tower, she thought, "I know not whether to rejoice or grieve at this sad war. I grieve that Minos is our enemy, but I rejoice at any cause that brings him to my sight. Perhaps he would be willing to grant us peace and receive me as hostage. I would fly down, if I could, and alight in his camp, and tell him that we yield ourselves to his mercy. Yet, that would be betraying my father! No! Rather would I never see Minos again. And still, sometimes it is the best thing for a city to be conquered when the conqueror is clement and generous. Minos certainly has right on his side. I think we shall be conquered. And if that must be the end of it, why should not love unbar the gates to him instead of war? Better spare delay and slaughter if we can. What if anyone should wound or kill Minos? No one would have the heart to do it, surely. Yet someone might. I will! I will surrender myself to him with my country as a dowry, and so put an end to the war. But how shall I do it? The gates are guarded and my father keeps the keys. He alone stands in my way. O, that it might please the gods to take him away. But why ask the gods to do it? Another woman, loving as I do, would remove with her own hands whatever stood in the way of her love. And can any woman dare more than I? I would encounter fire and sword for Minos. Here there is no need for fire and sword. I need only my father's purple lock. More precious than gold, it will give me all I wish."

She sat there until night came on and the whole palace slept. Silently, she crept to her father's bed-chamber and taking a dagger from the girdle of her robe, cut off his purple lock of hair. She unfastened the keys to the city from around his neck and stole to the gates. While the sentry dozed, she opened them a mere crack and quietly slipped through.

Stopped at the entrance to the enemy's camp, she demanded to be led to the king. Minos was sleeping, but arose when he received her message and permitted her to appear before him. "I am Scylla," she said, "the daughter of Nisus. I surrender to you my country and my father's house. I ask no reward but yourself. It is for love of you that I have betrayed my country. Look! Here is the purple lock from my father's head! With this I give you my father and his kingdom."

She held out her hand. Minos shrank back and refused to take the lock. "The gods destroy thee, infamous woman!" he cried. "You are the disgrace of our time! May neither earth nor sea give thee a resting place: Surely, my Crete, where Jupiter himself was cradled, shall not be polluted with such a monster!"

Turning from her in disgust, he gave orders that terms should be allowed to the conquered city. He bade his army to depart in friendliness, and ordered the fleet to sail home.

Scylla was frantic when she heard these commands. "Ungrateful man," she screamed, "is it thus you leave me? I have given you victory. I have sacrificed father and country for you! I am guilty, I confess, and deserve to die. But I shall not die by your hand!"

She threw herself to the ground and lay there while the invading army made ready for their departure. As the ships started to leave the shore, she leaped into the water and seizing the rudder of the

one which carried Minos, she was borne along, an unwelcome companion on their journey.

Back in the city Nisus learned of his daughter's treachery. He cursed her to the gods, and they changed him into a sea eagle and bade him follow her. He soared across the waters, and seeing Scylla clinging to the rudder below, he pounced down upon her, and struck her again and again with his beak and claws. In terror she let go of the ship and would have drowned if some kindly deity had not changed her into a bird. The sea eagle still cherishes his hatred and now when he sees her in his lofty flight, you may see him dart down upon her, with beak and claws, to take vengeance for the ancient crime.

CHAPTER XIII

Perseus Slays the Gorgon:

PERSEUS (pur'-suse) was the son of Jupiter and Danae. When he was born, his grandfather, Acrisius, consulted an oracle and prayed to know what the infant's fate would be. To his horror, the oracle answered that the child would one day slay him. Acrisius was terrified over this prophecy. He wanted to murder Perseus, but he was too tender-hearted to do the deed himself. He finally decided to shut up Danae and her baby in a chest and set them adrift on the sea. He secretly hoped they would be dashed to pieces on the rocks. Clinging to her baby in the dark, hot chest, Danae huddled in terror while the box whirled and dipped in the waves. It seemed days before they were washed upon the shores of Seriphus, where they were found by a fisherman. He took the mother and her baby to Polydectes, the king of the country, who took them into his own home and treated them with kindness. Here Perseus grew to manhood.

Not far from Seriphus, there lived a horrible monster named Medusa the Gorgon. She had once been a beautiful maiden whose hair was her chief glory, but, like Psyche who was also punished for her charms, Medusa had dared to vie in beauty with Minerva. Minerva in a rage turned her into a horrible figure, and changed her beautiful ringlets into hissing serpents. She became cruel and of so frightful an aspect that no living thing could behold her without being turned to stone. She dwelt in a foul, dank cavern and all around lay the stony figures of men and animals that had unfortunately chanced to catch a glimpse of her and had been petrified with the sight.

When Perseus became of age, Polydectes told him the story of the monster and begged him to attempt her conquest. Although Minerva had been the cause of Medusa's downfall, she favored Perseus and lent him her shield to take on his journey, while Mercury gave him his winged shoes so that he might travel with the speed of the wind.

As he neared the mouth of the cave where the dreadful maiden lived, Perseus turned his back lest he see Medusa and share the fate of others who had tried to kill her. Slowly and stealthily, he walked backwards, holding his shield before his eyes and guiding himself by the reflections in it. He entered the cave and beholding Medusa's head mirrored in the shining metal, he stopped in horror. Medusa lay asleep. Fastened securely to her scalp by the tips of their tails, noisome snakes writhed and twisted about her face and neck. Their breaths were fetid and their eyes winked evilly. Water dropped from the roof of the cave and the air was dank. In the half-light, Perseus saw hundreds of lizards and giant toads crawling over her body. The sight was so dreadful that he almost ran from it in terror, but remembering his vow to Polydectes who had raised him, he advanced slowly, keeping Medusa's image reflected in the shield. Closer and closer he crept until he stood within reach of the pestilential serpents of her hair. And then he struck. Her head fell to the ground.

After the slaughter of Medusa, Perseus, bearing with him the head of the Gorgon, flew far and wide, over land and sea. As night came on, he reached the western limit of the earth, where the sun goes down. He was tired and would have gladly rested here until morning. It was the realm of King Atlas, brother of Prometheus, who was more tremendous than any man on earth. Atlas was rich and had no neighbor or rival to dispute his supremacy of the land. His gardens were his chief pride. Here golden fruit hung from golden branches, half hid with golden leaves. Perseus presented himself to Atlas and said, "I come as a guest. If you honor illustrious descent, I claim Jupiter for my father. If you honor mighty deeds, I plead the conquest of the Gorgon. I seek rest and food."

Atlas was about to welcome him to his castle when he remembered an ancient prophecy which had warned him that a son of Jupiter would one day rob him of his golden apples. So, turning away, he answered, "Begone! Neither your false claims of glory nor parentage shall protect you!"

When Perseus did not move, Atlas turned on him and attempted to thrust him from the door. Perseus, finding the giant too strong for him, said, "Since you value my friendship so little, deign to accept a present!" And, turning his own face away, he held up the Gorgon's head. Atlas changed into stone. His beard and hair became forests, his arms and shoulders became cliffs; his head became a summit and his bones turned into rocks. Each part increased in bulk until he became a mountain and the gods willed that heaven with all its stars should rest upon his shoulders.

Perseus continued his flight and eventually arrived at the country of the Aethiopians, of which Cepheus (see'-fus) was king. His queen, Cassiopea had been so proud of her beauty that she had dared to compare herself to the sea-nymphs, which roused their indignation to such a degree that they sent a prodigious sea-monster to ravage the coast. Fishermen and ships were destroyed by the dreadful monster, and Cepheus in dismay consulted the oracle who directed him to sacrifice his daughter, Andromeda, to appease the deities. Weeping and sad, Cepheus ordered his beautiful daughter to be chained to a rock where the monster could find her and devour her. He kissed her tenderly and hastened away, fearing to look back.

At this moment, Perseus, flying far overhead, glanced down and saw the maiden. She was so pale and motionless, that if it had not been for her flowing tears and her hair that moved in the breeze, he would have taken her for a marble statue. He was startled at the sight and almost forgot to wave his wings. As he hovered over her, he said, "O maiden, undeserving of those chains, tell me, I beseech you, your name and the name of your country. Tell me why you are thus bound."

At first she was silent, half-frightened at the sight of the hero who floated in the wind above her. But seeing that he was not going to harm her, she told him her name and that of her country, and the punishment that had fallen on the land because of her mother's pride of beauty. Before she had finished speaking, a sound was heard far off on the water, and the sea-monster appeared with his head raised above the surface, cleaving the waves with his broad breast. Andromeda shrieked in terror, and her father and mother who were hiding not far away, rushed back to the rock. They stood near, wretched and helpless.

Perseus flew close to them and said, "There will be time enough for tears. This hour is all we have for rescue. My rank as the son of Jupiter and my renown as the slayer of Medusa might make me acceptable as a suitor. I will try to win her, if the gods will only favor me. If she be rescued by my valor, I demand that she be my reward."

The parents eagerly consented.

The monster was now within a stone's throw of Andromeda, when, with a sudden bound, Perseus

soared high into the air. As an eagle in flight sees a serpent basking in the sun and pounces on him, so the youth darted down upon the back of the monster and plunged his sword into its shoulder. Irritated by the wound the monster raised himself up and then plunged into the depths. Like a wild boar surrounded by a pack of barking dogs, it turned swiftly from side to side. Perseus stuck to its back and stuck it time and again with his sword, piercing its sides, its flanks and its tail. The brute spouted water and blood from its nostrils, and the wings of the hero were wet with them. He no longer dared trust them to carry his weight and he alighted on a rock which rose above the waves. As the monster floated near, he gave it a death stroke.

The people who had gathered on the shore shouted so that the hills re-echoed the sound. The parents, wild with joy, embraced their future son-in-law, and Andromeda was unchained and descended from the rock.

At the palace a banquet was spread for them, and joy and festivity ruled the land. But, suddenly, a noise was heard and Phineus (fee'-nuse), the betrothed of Andromeda, burst in and demanded the maiden as his own. It was in vain that Cepheus reasoned, "You should have claimed her when she lay bound to the rock, the monster's victim. The sentence of the gods dooming her to such a fate dissolved the engagement, as death itself would have done."

Phineus made no reply and hurled his javelin at Perseus. It missed its mark and fell to the floor. Perseus would have thrown his in turn, but the cowardly assailant ran and took shelter behind the altar. His act was a signal to his band who set upon the guests of Cepheus. They defended themselves and a general conflict ensued. The old king retreated from the scene after fruitless arguments and called the gods to witness that he was guiltless of this outrage on the rights of hospitality.

Perseus and his friends fought on, but the numbers of their assailants were too great for them. Then Perseus thought once more of the Gorgon's head. "I will make my enemy defend me," he said to himself. He called out, "If I have any friend here, let him turn away his eyes!"

He held Medusa's head high. "Seek not to frighten us with your tricks," a man cried, and raised his javelin to throw it. He was instantly turned to stone. Another was about to plunge his sword into the prostrate body of his foe when his arm stiffened and he could neither thrust it forward nor withdraw it. Men were petrified with their mouths open as they shouted in anger, and the swords of those still alive hit against the bodies of their enemies and broke.

Phineus, behind the altar, beheld the dreadful result of his injustice. He called aloud to his friends, but got no answer. He touched them and found them stone. Falling on his knees, he stretched out his hands to Perseus. "Take all," he begged. "Give me but my life!"

"Base coward," Perseus cried, "this much I will grant you. No weapon shall touch you. You shall be preserved in my house as a memorial of these events."

So saying, he held the Gorgon's head in front of Phineus, and in the very form in which he knelt with his hands outstretched and face half averted, he became fixed, a mass of stone!

CHAPTER XIV

The Sphinx:

LAIUS, the king of Thebes, was warned by an oracle that there was danger to his throne and to his life if his newborn son should be allowed to grow up. Frightened by this prediction, he took the sleeping child from its crib and gave it to a herdsman, with orders to murder the baby. The herdsman, moved with pity, yet not daring to disobey entirely, tied up the child by the feet and left him hanging to the branch of a tree. He was found by a peasant who carried him to his master and mistress. The kind couple adopted him and called him Oedipus (ed'-ih-pus), or Swollen-foot.

Many years later Laius traveled to Delphi accompanied only by one attendant. He turned into a narrow road near the city and met a young man who was driving a chariot. Laius ordered the young man out of his way and, because the lad was slow to obey,

the attendant killed one of his horses. The stranger, filled with rage at this injustice, slew both Laius and his attendant. The young man was Oedipus, who unknowingly became the slayer of his own father and fulfilled the prophecy made by the oracle.

Shortly after this event, the city of Thebes was molested by a monster which infested the main road leading into the city. This monster was called the Sphinx. It had the body of a lion and the upper part of a woman. It lay crouched on the top of a rock, and stopped all travelers who came that way, asking them a riddle with the condition that those who could solve it should pass safely, but those who failed should be killed. No one had yet succeeded in solving the riddle, and all had been slain. Oedipus was not daunted by these alarming accounts and boldly advanced to the trial. The Sphinx asked him, "What animal is that which in the morning goes on four feet, at noon on two feet, and in the evening on three feet?"

Oedipus replied, "Man, who in childhood creeps on hands and knees, in manhood walks erect, and in old age walks with the aid of a staff."

The Sphinx was so mortified at the solving of her riddle that she cast herself down from the rocks and perished. And the gratitude of the people of Thebes for their deliverance was so great that they made Oedipus their king.

CHAPTER XV

The Golden Fleece:

IN VERY ancient times there lived in Thessaly a king and queen named Athamas and Nephele (nef'-eh-lee). They had two children, a boy and a girl. After a time Athamas grew tired of his wife, divorced her and married another. Nephele worried about her children and, not wishing to leave them with a step-mother, took measures to send them away. Mercury came to her aid and gave her a ram with golden fleece on which she put the two children, trusting that the ram would carry them to a place of safety. The ram vaulted into the air with the children on his back and crossed the straits that divide Europe and Asia. Here the girl, whose name was Helle (hell'-ee), slipped from the ram's back and fell into the sea. And thereafter the straits were called the Hellespont. In modern times, they are called the Dardanelles. The ram continued his course until he reached the kingdom of Colchis (kol'-kis), on the eastern shore of the Black Sea, where he safely landed the boy Phrixus (frick'-sus). The king of the country, Aeetes (ay-ee'-teez), gladly welcomed the boy, and Phrixus asked that the ram be sacrificed to Jupiter. Its golden fleece was preserved and given to Aeetes. He placed it reverently in a consecrated grove under the care of a dragon who never slept.

There was another kingdom in Thessaly ruled over by a relative of King Athamas. The king, whose name was Aeson, grew tired of the cares of government and surrendered his crown to his brother Pelias, on the condition that he should reign only until Aeson's son, Jason, became of age. When Jason was grown up and came to demand the crown from his uncle, Pelias pretended to be willing to yield it, but suggested that Jason go on some glorious adventure before settling down to the worries of ruling a kingdom. He reminded him that the golden fleece was still in Colchis and that as it was the rightful property of their family, Jason should go in quest of it. The idea excited Jason and he made grand preparations for the expedition. At that time, the only way of navigation known to the Greeks was travel in small boats or canoes hollowed out from the trunks of trees. Jason, realizing that such boats would be too light for the long, hazardous trip, employed Argos to build him a vessel which would carry fifty men. It was considered a gigantic undertaking and took many months. When it was completed, Jason named the ship Argo in honor of the builder, and sent out an invitation to all the adventurous young men in Greece to join him on the expedition. He soon found himself the head of a band of bold youths, many of whom afterward were renowned among the heroes and demigods of Greece; Hercules, Orpheus and Nestor were among them. They called themselves the Argonauts.

The Argo with her crew of heroes left the shores of Thessaly and having stopped for supplies at the island of Lemnos, crossed over to Mysia (mish'-i-a) and then to Thrace. Here they consulted a wise old man who gave them instructions as to what course to follow. The entrance to the Euxine Sea was impeded by two small rocky islands. These islands were tossed and heaved about by the sea and occasionally came together, crushing and grinding to atoms any object that might be caught between them. They were called the Symplegades (sim-pleg'-a-deez), or Clashing Islands. The old man told the Argonauts how to pass this dangerous strait; when they reached the islands they released a dove from her cage and watched her as she passed between the rocks in safety. She lost only a few feathers from her tail. Then Jason and his men seized the favorable moment of the rebound, threw all their strength into the oars, and passed swiftly through, though the islands closed behind them and actually grazed their stern. They rowed close to the shore until they landed at the kingdom of Colchis.

Jason went before the king, Aeetes, who consented to give up the golden fleece, if Jason would yoke two fire-breathing bulls to the plough and sow more of the teeth of the dragon which Cadmus had slain. Aeetes knew very well that a crop of armed men would spring up who would turn against Jason. The young man agreed to sow the teeth and a time was set for making the experiment. Meanwhile, the Argonauts feasted and reveled.

As preparations were being made for the task, Jason met and fell in love with Medea, daughter of the king, and asked her to marry him as they stood before the altar of Hecate, who witnessed their oaths. Then Medea, who was skilled in the art of sorcery, gave him a charm which would protect him

against the fire-breathing bulls and the weapons of
the armed men.

At the appointed time, the people assembled at the
grove of Mars and the king assumed his royal seat,
while multitudes covered the nearby hillside. The
brazen-foot bulls rushed onto the field, breathing fire
from their nostrils that burned up grass and bushes
as they passed. The sound of their breathing was
like the roar of a furnace, and the smoke like that
of water upon quicklime. Everybody shrank back

at their approach, but Jason walked forth boldly to meet them. His friends turned away in fear for his life. He went near the beasts and soothed them with his voice, patted their necks and adroitly slipped on the yoke. When they were harnessed, he gently guided the plough. The Colchians were amazed. The Greeks shouted for joy. Jason next sowed the dragon's teeth and ploughed them in. And soon the crop of armed men sprang up, but no sooner had they reached the surface than they began to brandish their weapons and rush about Jason. The Argonauts trembled for their leader and even Medea feared her charm might not protect him. For a time Jason kept his assailants at bay with his sword and shield. Then, finding that their numbers were overwhelming, he resorted to the charm which Medea had taught him. He seized a stone and threw it into the midst of his foes. They immediately turned their arms against one another and soon there was not one of the dragon's brood left alive. The Greeks cheered their hero and Medea sat proud and happy at her father's side.

Jason, having won the right to the golden fleece, had to pass by the huge dragon to get it. Once more, Medea came to his aid. She gave him a powerful oil which Jason scattered near the monster. At the smell, he stood motionless for a moment, then shut his great eyes that had never been known to close before, turned over on his side, and went fast to sleep.

Jason seized the fleece and with his friends and Medea hastened to the Argo before Aeetes could dispute their departure. They sailed back to Thessaly and Jason delivered the fleece to Pelias and dedicated the Argo to Jupiter.

There was great rejoicing at the recovery of the golden fleece, and Jason longed for his father, Aeson, to share in the festivities. But Aeson was old and infirm and could not take part in them. Jason turned to Medea for help. "My spouse," he said, "would that your arts, whose powers have aided me, could do me one more service. Take some of the years from my life and add them to my father's."

Medea replied, "I shall not do it at such a cost, but if my art serves me, his life shall be lengthened without shortening yours."

The next full moon, she went forth all alone, while everyone slept. Not a breath stirred the foliage and all was still. She addressed her incantations to the stars and to the moon; she called on Hecate who represented the darkness and its terrors, and on Tellus, the goddess of the earth, who produced plants potent for enchantments. She invoked the gods of the woods and caverns, of mountains and valleys, of lakes and rivers, of winds and vapors. As she spoke, the stars shone brighter, and presently a chariot descended through the air, drawn by flying serpents. She stepped into it and was borne aloft to distant regions where strange plants grew. She spent nine days and nine nights selecting a few from the thousands that she saw, and during this time, she did not enter a door, nor did she sleep under a roof, nor speak to any mortal.

She next erected two altars, one to Hecate and the other to Hebe, goddess of youth, and sacrificed a black sheep to the goddesses, pouring them libations of milk and wine. She begged Pluto and his stolen bride, Proserpina, not to take the old man's life. Then she directed that Aeson should be led forth and she put him to sleep with a potent charm. She laid him on a bed of herbs, like one dead. Throughout these ceremonies, Jason and all the others were kept away so that no profane eyes should look upon her mysteries. With her hair streaming, she moved around the altars three times, dipped flaming twigs in the blood of the sheep and laid them on the altars to burn. She prepared a huge cauldron and in it she put magic herbs, with seeds and flowers of acrid juices, stones from the distant East and sand from the shore of the all-surrounding ocean. She put in hoar frost, gathered by moonlight, a screech owl's head and wings, and the entrails of a wolf. She added fragments of the shells of tortoises, and the liver of stags, the head and beak of a crow that outlives nine generations of men. These with many other things so weird that they had no name she boiled together, stirring them up with a wild olive branch. And when the branch was taken out of the mixture, it instantly became green! Before long it was covered with leaves and a plentiful growth of young olives. As the liquor boiled and bubbled, grass sprouted on the ground where the liquid fell.

When all was ready, Medea cut the old man's throat and let out all his blood and poured into his mouth and into the wound the juices of her cauldron. Slowly his hair and beard changed from white to a rich dark black; he lost his paleness and his body grew vigorous and robust. Aeson was amazed when he awoke to find that he looked as he had forty years ago.

When Pelias's daughters saw what Medea had done

for Aeson, they begged her to restore youth to their own father. But, Medea, remembering that Pelias had kept Jason from ruling his kingdom while he sent him on the dangerous quest for the golden fleece, only pretended to agree. She prepared her cauldron as before, and at her request an old sheep was brought and plunged into it. Very soon a bleating was heard in the kettle, and a lamb jumped forth and ran frisking away to the meadows. The daughters of Pelias saw this experiment and were delighted, and appointed a time for their father to undergo the same operation. But Medea put water and a few simple herbs in it, instead. And in the night, she and the daughters entered the bedchamber of the old king while he and his guards slept soundly. The daughters stood by the bedside, but hesitated to cut their father's throat until Medea jeered at them for their irresolution. Turning away their heads, they struck random blows. Pelias, starting from his sleep, cried out, "My daughters, what are you doing? Will you kill your father?"

Their hearts failed them and the weapons fell from their hands, but Medea struck him a final blow. His daughters carried him to the altar and placed him in the cauldron, and Medea hastened to depart in her serpent-drawn chariot. She escaped, but was to live to repent her evil deed. Jason turned away from her in disgust and desired to marry Creusa, princess of Corinth. Medea, enraged at his ingratitude after the help she had given him, sent a poisoned robe as a gift to the princess and then set fire to the palace. She escaped once more in her serpent-drawn chariot and fled to Athens, where she married King Aegeus (ee'-juse), the father of Theseus.

CHAPTER XVI

Meleager and the Wild Boar:

ONE of the heroes of the Argonautic expedition was Meleager. He was the son of Oeneus (ee'-nuse) and Althea, king and queen of Calydon. Shortly after he was born, his mother saw the three Fates spinning the fatal thread of his destiny, and heard them say that the child's life should last no longer than a brand which was then burning on the hearth. Althea seized the brand from the fire and quenched it in a bowl of water. She hid it and carefully preserved it for years, while Meleager grew to manhood.

Although Oeneus, his father, was a religious man and made daily offerings to the gods, he, by chance, omitted to pay due honors to Diana. The goddess was indignant at this neglect and sent a wild boar of enormous size to destroy the fields of Calydon. It was a dreadful creature with bristles that stood out like threatening spears, eyes that shone with blood and fire, and tusks as large as those of an Indian elephant. He trampled on the growing corn, tore down the vines and olive trees, and scattered the flocks of sheep and herds of cattle. Traps and snares were set for him, but he could not be captured.

Meleager, in desperation, called on the heroes of Greece to join in a bold hunt for the ravenous monster. Theseus and his friends—Pirithous (pie-rith'-o-us), Jason, Peleus who became the father of Achilles, Telamon, the father of Ajax, Nestor who later bore arms with Achilles and Ajax in the Trojan War—these and many more joined in the enterprise. And with them came Atalanta, the daughter of Iasius, king of Arcadia. A buckle of polished gold held her belt, an ivory quiver hung on her left shoulder, and her left hand carried the bow.

When Atalanta was a little girl, the oracle had spoken to her thus: "Atalanta, do not marry. Marriage will be your ruin." Terrified by this prophecy, she had shunned the society of men and had devoted herself to the sports of the chase. She was tall and beautiful and it was not surprising that Meleager fell in love with her at first sight.

After a great feast at the palace, the young men with Atalanta made ready for the hunt. They rode near the monster's lair and stretched strong nets from tree to tree. They untied their dogs, and tried to find the footprints of their quarry in the grass. The woods where the boar roamed descended sharply to marshy ground, and the animal, hearing the approach of the hunters, fled down the slope and hid among the reeds. As his pursuers drew near, he rushed forth against them. One after another, the men were thrown and slain. Jason threw his spear with a prayer to Diana for success, and the favoring goddess allowed the weapon to touch the boar but not to wound him. Nestor, rushed by the maddened beast, sought safety in a tree. Telamon charged, but caught his foot and fell. Atalanta's arrow was the first to taste the monster's blood. It made only a slight wound, but Meleager, seeing it, called out proudly to the others. Then Anceus, excited to envy by the praise given the girl, loudly proclaimed his own valor and defied the boar and the goddess who sent it. He charged and the beast laid him low with a mortal wound. Theseus threw his lance, and it caught in the branch of a tree. Jason's dart missed its object and killed one of the dogs.

At last, Meleager, fired by the sight of Atalanta's arrow which still quivered in the boar's side, drove his spear into the monster. The animal gave a frightful cry, and, falling forward, died.

A shout rose from those around. They congratulated the conquerer, crowding to touch his hand. He placed his foot on the head of the slain boar, and turning to Atalanta, bestowed on her the head and the rough hide which were the trophies of his success. At this gesture, there were mutters of disapproval from the hunters. Plexippus and Toxeus (tocks'-use), uncles of Meleager, especially opposed his action, and snatched the trophy away from the maiden. Meleager, trembling with rage at the wrong done himself, and still more at the insult offered to Atalanta, forgot the claims of kindred and plunged his sword into the offenders' hearts.

As Althea bore gifts of gratitude to the temples for the victory of her son, she saw the bodies of her murdered brothers. She shrieked and beat her breast and hastened to change the garments of rejoicing for those of mourning. And when she learned that her own son was the cause of their deaths, her grief gave way to a desire for revenge. She went to the place where the fatal brand that the Fates had linked with Meleager's life lay hidden. And bringing it forth, she commanded that a fire be prepared. Screaming curses on her son, four times she tried to place the brand upon the roaring flames, and four times she drew back. The feelings of the mother and the sister fought for her soul. She grew pale with the thought of what she was about to do, then flushed with anger as she remembered the cruel death of her brothers. Like a boat driven in one direction by the wind, and in the opposite direction by the tide, Althea's mind hung suspended in uncertainty.

Her rage finally overcame her love for Meleager and she approached the fire once more with the brand of death. "Turn, ye Furies, goddesses of punishment!" she cried. "Turn to behold the sacrifice I bring! Shall Oeneus rejoice in his victorious son while the house of Thestius is desolate? Yet, to what deed am I borne along? My brothers, forgive a mother's weakness! My hand fails me! He deserves death but I cannot destroy him! But shall he then live, and triumph, and reign over Calydon, while you, my brothers, wander unavenged among the shades? No! Thou hast lived, Meleager, by my gift. Die, now, for thine own crime! Return the life which twice I gave thee, first at birth, again when I snatched this brand from the flames! Alas! Evil is the conquest, but, brothers, ye have conquered!"

And, turning away her face, she threw the fatal wood upon the burning pile.

It gave, or seemed to give, a deadly groan.

At this moment, Meleager was walking through the woods with Atalanta by his side, surrounded by the heroes who acclaimed him. As the brand that gave him life touched the fire, he felt a sudden pang. His heart felt as though a fire raged in his breast. With courageous pride, he walked on fighting the pain that was destroying him, until, as the brand grew white hot in the flames, he fell to the ground. With his last breath, he called upon his aged father, his brother, his beloved sisters, and his adored Atalanta. He cried out to his mother, the unknown cause of his fate. The flames increased and the pain of the hero increased with them. Both subsided. Both were quenched. The brand was ashes and the life of Meleager was breathed forth to the wandering winds.

For a long time, Althea stood and watched the dying embers. Then, overcome with grief, she thrust a dagger through her heart and fell forward into the ashes. The sisters of Meleager mourned their brother with uncontrollable grief. And Diana, pitying the sorrows of the house that once had aroused her anger, turned them into birds.

CHAPTER XVII

The Twelve Labors of Hercules:

THE day Hercules was born, Juno declared war against him. He was the son of Jupiter and Alcmene (alk-mee′-neh), and Juno, always hostile to the offspring of Jupiter by mortal mothers, sent two serpents to destroy him as he lay in his cradle. Hercules seized the snakes and strangled them with his own hands. Now, before his birth, it had been destined that the baby born on a certain day should rule over the descendants of Perseus. Juno, fearful that this honor would fall on Hercules, retarded his coming and hastened the birth of Eurystheus (u-ris′-thuse) so that he would fulfill the prophecy and become ruler. When the serpents failed to kill Hercules, Juno abandoned her attempts and bound him in servitude to Eurystheus instead, compelling him to perform all her favorite's commands. The tasks set Hercules were so dangerous that she hoped the young man would be slain.

Eurystheus ordered Hercules to engage on a succession of desperate adventures, which are called the "Twelve Labors of Hercules."

At this time, the valley of Nemea was inhabited by a terrible lion. He was large and fierce and had overcome all the hunters who had been sent to capture him. Eurystheus bade Hercules to bring him the skin of this monster. He went alone and sought the animal in its lair. Calling him forth, he set on the beast with a club, but his blows fell on the lion's thick skull in vain. Then Hercules caught him and strangled him with his bare hands as he had the serpents. He returned carrying the dead lion on his shoulders. Eurystheus was so frightened at the sight of it and at the proof of the prodigious strength of the hero, that he ordered him to deliver the accounts of his exploits outside the town in the future.

His next labor was the slaughter of the Hydra. This monster ravaged the country of Argos, and dwelt in a swamp near the well of Amymone. The well had been discovered by Amymone when the country was suffering from a dreadful drought, and

Neptune, who loved the maiden, had permitted her to touch a rock with his trident, and a spring of three outlets burst forth. Here the Hydra took up his position, and Hercules was sent to destroy him. The Hydra had nine heads, and his middle head was immortal. Accompanied by his faithful servant, Iolaus, Hercules set forth to vanquish the monster. It lay near the spring, polluting the clear waters, and devouring any person who came to fill his pitcher at the fountain. Hercules attacked the Hydra savagely, striking at his heads with his club, but each time he knocked off a head, two new ones grew forth. At length, with the help of Iolaus, he tied up the monster and burned away its heads, and buried the ninth and immortal one under a huge rock.

Eurystheus was enraged that his rival had performed another task successfully and sent him off immediately to clean the Augean (o-jee'-an) stables. Augeas (o-jee'-as), king of Elis, had a herd of three thousand oxen, whose stalls had not been cleaned for thirty years. Filth lay piled up almost to the oxen's heads and Hercules, seeing the state of the stables, was dismayed. It did not seem possible that he could clean them before nightfall. Two rivers, the Alpheus and the Peneus, flowed near by, and Hercules diverted them from their beds and brought them through the stables. The clear rushing waters swept all the dirt before them, and at sundown the stables were washed and in order.

His next labor was of a more delicate kind. Admeta, the daughter of Eurystheus, longed to own the girdle of the queen of the Amazons, and Eurystheus ordered Hercules to go and get it for her. The Amazons were a nation of women. They were very warlike and held several flourishing cities. It was their custom to bring up only their female children. The boys were either sent away to neighboring nations or put to death. On this adventure, Hercules was accompanied by a number of young men who had volunteered to aid him on his quest. They at last reached the country of the Amazons. Hippolyta (hih-pol'-i-tah), the queen, received them kindly, and consented to give him her girdle. But Juno, enraged that the hero was accomplishing his labor so easily, took the form of an Amazon and persuaded the powerful women of the country that Hercules was carrying off their queen. They armed themselves and came in great numbers down to the ship. There, Hercules, thinking that Hippolyta had betrayed him, killed her and took her girdle to Eurystheus.

Then, Eurystheus asked him to bring home the oxen of Geryon (jee'-ri-on), a monster with three bodies, who dwelt on the island of Erytheia (err-ih-thee'-ya), the Red, so called because it lay at the west under the rays of the setting sun. After crossing several countries, Hercules at length reached the frontiers of Libya and Europe, where he raised the two mountains of Calpe and Abyla as monuments of his progress. These mountains formed the straits of Gibraltar and were called the Pillars of Hercules.

The monster he had been sent to kill was guarded by the giant Eurytion and his two-headed dog, and Hercules killed the giant and his dog and brought away the oxen safely to Eurystheus.

The most difficult labor of all was getting the golden apples of the Hesperides (hes-per'-ih-deez), for Hercules did not know where to find them. These were the apples which Juno had received at her wedding from the goddess of the Earth. She had entrusted them to the keeping of the daughters of Hesperus who were assisted by a faithful dragon. After searching throughout the world, Hercules finally arrived at Mount Atlas in Africa. Atlas, who bore the weight of the heavens on his shoulders, was the father of the Hesperides, and Hercules thought that he might, if any could, find the apples and bring them to him. But how could he send Atlas away from his post, and who would bear up the heavens while he was gone? In his mighty strength, Hercules took the burden on his own shoulders and sent Atlas to seek the apples. The giant Titan was only too glad to be released from his eternal punishment and gladly went on the search. He called to his daughters who answered him, and they gave him the precious apples. Atlas reluctantly returned and took the heavens on his shoulders once more, and Hercules took the apples to Eurystheus.

On his travels, Hercules encountered Antaeus (an-tee´-us), the son of Terra, the Earth. He was a mighty giant and wrestler, whose strength was invincible so long as he remained in contact with his mother Earth. He compelled all strangers who passed through his country to wrestle with him, on condition that if conquered, which they all were, they should be put to death. Hercules fought him and, finding that it was of no avail to throw him, for he always rose with renewed strength from every fall, he lifted him up from the earth and strangled him in the air.

In the pursuit of his tasks, Hercules had many

dangerous adventures. He had met the giant Cacus
(kay'-kus) who inhabited a cave on Mount Aven-
tine and plundered the surrounding country. When
Hercules was driving home the oxen of Geryon,
Cacus stole part of the cattle while the hero slept.
He had dragged them off backward by their tails,
that their footprints might not serve to show where
they had been driven. Their tracks all seemed to
show that they had gone in the opposite direction.

Hercules was deceived by this ruse and would have failed to find his oxen, if it had not happened that in driving the remainder of the herd past the cave where the stolen ones were concealed, he heard them lowing. Entering the cave, he discovered the oxen and Cacus was slain.

Hercules was next sent to bring Cerberus from the lower world. Cerberus was a gigantic, three-headed dog who guarded the gates of Hades. Pluto gave his permission to carry the beast to the upper air, providing Hercules could do so without the use of weapons. Accompanied by Mercury and Minerva, Hercules journeyed to the realms of darkness and, in spite of the monster's struggling, he seized him, held him fast, and carried him to Eurystheus, and afterwards brought him back again. While he was in Hades, he obtained the release of Theseus, his admirer and imitator, who had been kept prisoner there for an unsuccessful attempt to carry off Proserpina.

Worn out by his adventures which had taxed his tremendous strength to the utmost, Hercules became nervous and easily roused to anger. And, one day, in a fit of madness, he killed his friend Iphitus. He was condemned for this offense to become the slave of Queen Omphale for three years. While in this service, the hero's spirit seemed broken. He refused to talk of his heroic exploits and was content with the company of the hand-maidens of Omphale, assisting them in their spinning and even allowing their queen to wear his lion's skin. When the service was ended, he married Dejanira and lived happily with her for three years. Once, when he was traveling with his wife, they came to a river, across which the Centaur Nessus carried travelers for a stated fee. Hercules forded the river himself but gave Dejanira to Nessus to be carried across. Nessus attempted to run away with her, but Hercules heard her cries and shot an arrow into the heart of Nessus. The dying Centaur told Dejanira to take a portion of his blood and keep it as a charm to preserve the love of her husband.

Dejanira did so, and before long fancied she had occasion to use it. In one of his conquests, Hercules had taken prisoner a fair maiden named Iole (eye'-o-lee). When he was about to offer sacrifices to the gods in honor of his victory, he sent to his wife for a white robe to use. Dejanira, jealous of Iole, thinking it a good opportunity to try her love spell, steeped the garment in the blood of Nessus. She took good care to wash out all traces of it, but the magic power remained. And as soon as the garment became warm on the body of Hercules, the poison penetrated into all his limbs and caused the most intense agony. In his frenzy, he seized Lichas (lee'-kas), who had brought him the fatal robe, and hurled him into the sea. He wrenched off the garment, but it stuck to his flesh, and with it he tore away whole pieces of his body. In this frightful state, he embarked on a ship and sailed home. Dejanira, on seeing what she had unwittingly done, hung herself. Hercules, realizing that he was dying, ascended Mount Oeta (ee'-ta). He built a funeral pyre of trees, and giving his bows and arrows to Philoctetes (fill-ock-tee'-tez), he laid down on the pyre, his head resting on his club, and his lion's skin spread over him. With a face as serene as if he were taking his place at a festal board, he commanded Philoctetes to apply the torch. The great hero was weary. His deeds of strength lay behind him, and he heroically lent his body to the clean flames.

The gods felt troubled at seeing the champion of the earth brought to his end. Jupiter addressed them. "I am pleased to see your concern," he said, "and am gratified to perceive that I am the ruler of a loyal people, and that my brave son enjoys your favor. For although your interest in him arises from his noble deeds, yet it is not the less gratifying to me. But now I say to you, fear not! He who conquered all else is not to be conquered by those flames which you see blazing on Mount Oeta. Only his mother's share in him can perish. What he derived from me is immortal. I shall take him, dead to earth, to the heavenly shores, and I ask of you all to receive him kindly. If any of you feel grieved at his attaining this honor, no one can deny that he has deserved it."

The gods all gave their consent. Juno heard the words with some displeasure, yet not enough to make her regret the decision of her husband.

So when the flames had consumed the mother's share of Hercules, the divine part rose from the flames with an awful dignity. Jupiter enveloped him in a cloud and took him up in a chariot drawn by four horses to dwell among the stars. And as he took his place in heaven, the shoulders of Atlas bent lower with the added weight. Juno, now reconciled to him, gave him her daughter Hebe in marriage. He dwelt, a hero among the gods, until the end of time. The heavy burden that he had borne since his birth was lost in his earthly death, and he lived forever after, brave and strong, with youth's bright goddess at his side.

CHAPTER XVIII

Theseus and the Minotaur:

THESEUS (thee'-suse) was the son of Aegeus (ee'-jus), king of Athens, and of Aethra, daughter of the king of Troezen (tree'-zen). He was brought up at Troezen, and when he reached the age of manhood was to proceed to Athens and present himself to his father. Before his birth, Aegeus had placed his own sword and shoes under a large stone and told his wife to send his son to him when he became strong enough to roll away the stone and take the sword and shoes from under it. When she thought that the time had come, his mother led Theseus to the stone, and he rolled it aside with ease. As the roads were infested with robbers, his grandfather, the king of Troezen, urged him earnestly to take the shorter and safer way to his father's country, which was to go by sea. But the youth, feeling in himself the spirit and soul of a hero, was eager to emulate Hercules, with whose fame all Greece then rang. He wished to destroy the evil-doers and monsters that oppressed the country, and determined to take the more perilous and adventurous journey by land.

His first day's journey brought him to Epidaurus (ep-i-do'-rus) where Periphetes dwelt, the son of Vulcan. This ferocious savage always went about armed with a club of iron, and all travelers stood in terror of his violence. When he saw Theseus approach, he set upon him viciously, but he soon fell beneath the blows of the young hero, who took possession of his club and carried it ever afterwards as a memento of his first victory. Several similar contests with the petty tyrants and marauders of the country followed, in all of which Theseus was victorious. One of these monsters was called Procrustes (pro-krus'-teez), or the Stretcher. He had an iron bedstead on which he tied all travelers who fell into his hands. If they were shorter than the bed, he stretched their limbs to make them fit it; if they were longer than the bed, he cut off their feet and ankles. Theseus tied him to the bed and cut off his head to make him fit it.

Having overcome all the perils of the road, Theseus reached Athens at last, where new dangers awaited him. Medea, the sorceress who had fled from Corinth after her separation from Jason, had become the wife of Aegeus, the father of Theseus. Knowing by her magic arts who he was and fearing the loss of her influence with her husband if Theseus should be acknowledged as his son, she filled the mind of Aegeus with suspicions of the young stranger. She whispered to Aegeus that the youth had come to poison him, and that he, in turn, should administer a cup of poison to Theseus. When Theseus stepped forward to take it, Aegeus caught sight of his own sword hanging at the hero's side, and striking the fatal cup to the floor, he embraced the boy and called upon everyone to witness that he had found his son. Medea, once more detected in her villainies, fled the country and went to Asia, where the country afterwards called Medea received its name from her.

The Athenians were at that time in deep affliction on account of the tribute which they were forced to pay to Minos, king of Crete. Every year seven youths and seven maidens were sent to be devoured by the Minotaur, a monster with a bull's body and a human head. It was a horrid beast, strong and fierce, and was kept in a labyrinth which had been constructed by Daedalus. The labyrinth was so artfully designed that whoever entered it could never find his way out unassisted. Paths led into paths, and all of them seemingly led nowhere. Here the Minotaur roamed and was fed with human victims.

Every year when the time came for the youths and maidens to be delivered to the monster, the country was plunged into mourning. Mothers trembled lest their beautiful daughters or brave sons should be chosen to feed the dreadful creature, and the houses of the entire populace were draped in black as the procession of young people bravely set out for the labyrinth. When Theseus arrived in Athens, the time was approaching for the sacrifice. He noticed the sad faces of the people of the city and asked his father to tell him the cause of their sorrow. Aegeus reluctantly told him the story. Theseus, indignant at the cruel and useless sacrifice, resolved to deliver his countrymen from the calamity or die in the attempt. The youths and maidens were drawn by lot every year, but Theseus, in spite of the entreaties of his father, offered himself as one of the victims.

The morning for their departure dawned, and Theseus joined the weeping, shivering group. They were dressed in deep black, but Theseus had arrayed himself in gay colors, confident of victory. The ship which was to carry them to their destination had black sails, and Theseus promised his father that he would change the sails to white if he returned victorious.

When they arrived in Crete, the youths and maidens were exhibited before Minos, and Ariadne (ar-i-ad'-nee), the daughter of the king, saw Theseus and fell in love with him. She furnished him with a sword and with a spool of thread. She instructed him to fasten the thread to a stone as he entered the labyrinth and unwind it as he made his way into the maze, keeping it firmly grasped in his hand so that he could guide himself back to the daylight once more.

Cheered by these gifts, the young people entered the dark, wet caves. They clung together while Theseus fastened the thread securely to a jutting rock, and then, walking one behind the other, they followed the first path. Around and around they traveled, their ears alert for the slightest sound which would warn them of the approach of the monster. It was pitch dark, and Theseus was careful of the thread lest it catch on a sharp corner and break off. They wandered for hours, too cold and frightened to sit down. Their eyes became accustomed to the darkness and they could make out the tall grey walls and hundreds of paths winding in the half-light. There was an odor of decay in the air, and they saw the white bones of the victims of other years lying on the ground.

Suddenly, they heard a tremendous bellowing and the stamping of angry feet. It was the Minotaur, ravenous from his year's fast, and anxious to partake of the sweet blood of the youths and maidens. At the sound, there were screams of horror from the victims. Theseus begged them to be calm and, ordering them to a place of comparative safety in the rocks, he advanced alone to meet the Minotaur. He saw the monster's head as it turned the corner. Its beard was caked with the blood of years. Its mouth dripped in anticipation of the feast that awaited it. It uttered wild cries which resembled the bellowings of a bull and the roars of an insane human. As it caught sight of Theseus, it galloped forward ready to crunch him in its powerful jaws, trample him with its cloven hoofs, and devour him. With one quick movement, Theseus stepped forward and plunged his sword into the creature's breast. Maddened, the Minotaur reared and would have brought its feet down on Theseus's head, had not the hero ducked and stabbed him time and time again. When the monster lay dead, the young people threw their arms around one another in a frenzy of joy, and following the precious thread, made their way out of the labyrinth.

They silently crept to their ship which lay in the harbor, and, with Ariadne, set sail for Athens. On their way home, they stopped at the island of Naxos where Theseus dreamed that Minerva appeared to him and commanded him to abandon Ariadne. He awoke and roused his companions, leaving Ariadne asleep on the island.

On approaching the coast of Attica, Theseus forgot the signal and neglected to raise the white sails. Aegeus, thinking his son had perished, put an end to his own life. Thus, Theseus became king of Athens.

Some time later, Theseus led an expedition against the Amazons. They had not yet recovered from their battle with Hercules when he descended on them and carried off their queen, Hippolyta. In revenge, the Amazons invaded Athens, and the final battle between the two forces was fought in the heart of the city.

Theseus had as a friend a hero named Pirithous (pie-rith'-o-us). They had met as enemies when Pirithous entered the plains of Marathon and carried

off the herds of the king of Athens. Theseus went to repel the plunderers, but the moment Pirithous beheld the slayer of the Minotaur, he was seized with admiration and stretched out his hand as a token of peace. "Judge me," he cried. "What satisfaction dost thou require?"

"Thy friendship!" Theseus called back. And they swore undying fidelity. They continued to be true brothers in arms. Each of them desired to wed a daughter of Jupiter. Theseus fixed his choice on Helen, then a child, who afterwards became celebrated as the cause of the Trojan War, and with the aid of his friend he carried her off. Pirithous aspired to the wife of the monarch of Erebus, Proserpina. And, Theseus, aware of the danger, accompanied the ambitious lover in his descent to the underworld. Pluto seized them and set them on an enchanted rock at his palace gate, where they remained until Hercules arrived and liberated Theseus, leaving Pirithous to his fate.

After the death of Hippolyta, the captured Amazon queen, Theseus married Phaedra (fee'-dra), daughter of Minos, king of Crete. Theseus had grown old, and Phaedra fell in love with his son, Hippolytus (hih-pol'-i-tus), a youth endowed with all the graces and virtues of his father. She adored him, but he repulsed her advances and her love was changed to hate. She used her influence over her infatuated husband and caused him to be jealous of his son. Theseus called down the judgment of Neptune upon the youth. And as Hippolytus was driving his chariot along the shore one day, a sea-monster raised himself above the waters and frightened the horses. They ran away and dashed the chariot to bits. Hippolytus was killed, but by Diana's assistance Aesculapius (es-ku-lay'-pi-us), a renowned physician, restored him to life. Diana took Hippolytus away from his father and his false stepmother and placed him in Italy under the protection of the nymph Egeria.

Theseus at length lost the favor of his people, and retired to the court of Lycomedes, king of Scyros, who at first received him kindly and afterwards treacherously slew him. Many, many years later, the Athenian general Cimon (ki'-mon) discovered the place where the hero was buried and brought his body back to Athens. His coffin was reverently placed in a temple called the Theseum, erected in his honor.

CHAPTER XIX

The Flight of Icarus:

WHEN Theseus escaped from the labyrinth, King Minos flew into a rage with its builder, Daedalus (dead'-a-lus), and ordered him shut up in a high tower that faced the lonely sea. In time, with the help of his young son, Icarus (ick'-a-rus), Daedalus managed to escape from the tower, only to find himself a prisoner on the island. Several times he tried by bribery to stow away on one of the vessels sailing from Crete, but King Minos kept strict watch over them and no ships were allowed to sail without being carefully searched.

Daedalus was an ingenious artist and was not discouraged by his failures. "Minos may control the land and sea," he said, "but he does not control the air. I will try that way."

He called his son Icarus to him and told the boy to gather up all the feathers he could find on the rocky shore. As thousands of gulls soared over the island, Icarus soon collected a hugh pile of feathers. Daedalus then melted some wax and made a skeleton in the shape of a bird's wing. The smallest feathers he pressed into the soft wax and the large ones he tied on with thread. Icarus played about on the beach happily while his father worked, chasing the feathers that blew away in the strong wind that swept the island and sometimes taking bits of the wax and working it into strange shapes with his fingers.

It was fun making the wings. The sun shone on the bright feathers, the breezes ruffled them. When they were finished Daedalus fastened them to his shoulders and found himself lifted upwards where he hung poised in the air. Filled with excitement, he made another pair for his son. They were smaller than his own, but strong and beautiful.

Finally, one clear, wind-swept morning, the wings were finished and Daedalus fastened them to Icarus's shoulders and taught him how to fly. He bade him watch the movements of the birds, how they soared and glided overhead. He pointed out the slow, graceful sweep of their wings as they beat the air steadily, without fluttering. Soon Icarus was sure that he, too, could fly and, raising his arms up and down, skirted over the white sand and even out over the waves, letting his feet touch the snowy foam as the water thundered and broke over the sharp rocks. Daedalus watched him proudly but with misgivings. He called Icarus to his side, and putting his arm round the boy's shoulders, said, "Icarus, my son, we are about to make our flight. No human being has ever traveled through the air before, and I want you to listen carefully to my instructions. Keep at a moderate height, for if you fly too low the fog and spray will clog your wings, and if you fly too high the heat will melt the wax that holds them together. Keep near me and you will be safe."

He kissed Icarus and fastened the wings more securely to his son's shoulders. Icarus, standing in the bright sun, the shining wings drooping gracefully from his shoulders, his golden hair wet with spray and his eyes bright and dark with excitement, looked like a lovely bird. Daedalus's eyes filled with tears and turning away he soared into the sky, calling to Icarus to follow. From time to time, he looked back to see that the boy was safe and to note how he managed his wings in his flight. As they flew across the land to test their prowess before setting out across the dark wild sea, ploughmen below stopped their work and shepherds gazed in wonder, thinking Daedalus and Icarus were gods.

Father and son flew over Samos (say'-mos) and Delos (dee'-los) which lay to their left, and Lebinthus, which lay on their right. Icarus, beating his wings in joy, felt the thrill of the cool wind on his face and the clear air above and below him. He flew higher and higher up into the blue sky until he reached the clouds. His father saw him and called out in alarm. He tried to follow him, but he was heavier and his wings would not carry him. Up and up Icarus soared, through the soft moist clouds and out again toward the glorious sun. He was bewitched by a sense of freedom and beat his wings frantically so that they would carry him higher and higher to heaven itself. The blazing sun beat down on the wings and softened the wax. Small feathers fell from the wings and floated softly down, warning Icarus to stay his flight and glide to earth. But the enchanted boy did not notice them until the sun became so hot that the largest feathers dropped off and he began to sink. Frantically he fluttered his arms, but no feathers remained to hold the air. He cried out to his father but his voice was submerged in the blue waters of the sea, which has forever after been called by his name.

Daedalus, crazed by anxiety, called back to him, "Icarus! Icarus, my son, where are you?" At last **he** saw the feathers floating from the sky and soon his son plunged through the clouds into the sea. Daedalus hurried to save him, but it was too late. He gathered the boy in his arms and flew to land, the tips of his wings dragging in the water from the double burden they bore. Weeping bitterly, he buried his small son and called the land Icaria in his memory.

Then, with a flutter of wings, he once more took to the air, but the joy of his flight was gone and his victory over the air was bitter to him. He arrived safely in Sicily where he built a temple to Apollo and hung up his wings as an offering to the god, and in the wings he pressed a few bright feathers he had found floating on the water where Icarus fell. And he mourned for the bird-like son who had thrown caution to the winds in the exaltation of his freedom from the earth.

CHAPTER XX

Bacchus, God of Wine:

BACCHUS (back'-us) was the son of Jupiter and Semele, who was the daughter of Cadmus and Harmonia and the granddaughter of Venus. When he was born, Juno grew jealous of Semele and thought of a way to destroy her. The goddess disguised herself as Beroe (ber'-o-ee), Semele's old nurse, and questioned the lovely young woman about the father of her child. "You say he is Jupiter," she sighed. "And I hope for your sake that this is so. I have my doubts. Men are not always what they claim to be. If he is truly Jupiter, make him give some proof of it. Tell him to come before you arrayed in all his splendor, such as he wears in heaven. Then you will be sure."

By continual nagging, she finally persuaded Semele to beg a favor from Jupiter the next time he descended to earth. Slyly, Semele did not tell him what the favor would be, but merely pleaded with him to grant it. Jupiter was amused at her childishness and told her that she could have whatever her heart desired, and he swore by the River Styx, a terrible oath, that he would grant her request. As she began to speak and he realized what she asked of him, he tried to stop her, but the words once out of her mouth could not be unsaid. He kissed her tenderly and in despair returned to Olympus. There he sadly opened the golden chest which contained his many splendors. He carefully selected a few garments. The terrors he sometimes wore when subduing giants he left in the chest, and only chose his lesser and friendlier robes, hoping that Semele could withstand their brilliance. Then, descending to earth, he entered her chamber. He shone with immortal radiance, and Semele, lifting her eyes, beheld him. Her human body could not endure the splendor of his presence and she was burned to ashes.

Jupiter discarded his splendid dress, and carried the infant Bacchus away to the Nysaean nymphs. They guarded him carefully through his infancy and childhood and were rewarded by Jupiter who placed them among the stars. They were called the Hyades (hie'-a-deez).

Bacchus grew up and lived in peace on the slopes of a fertile hill where grapes grew in abundance. He cultivated the vines and soon discovered a method of extracting the juice from the fruit. Then, Juno, still hating him because of the jealousy she had borne his mother, sought him out and struck him with madness, driving him from his home. He became a wanderer, roaming all over the earth until he reached Phrygia. There the goddess Rhea (ree'-a), the mother of Jupiter, found him and took pity on him. She nursed him tenderly and cured him of his madness. She taught him her religious rites and when he was restored to health he set out for a tour through Asia, where he taught the people the cultivation of the vine. His triumph was great in Asia, and after a few years he returned to Greece and tried to introduce his teachings there. But the people were afraid. The juice of the wine, they said, drove men mad.

As he approached Thebes, Pentheus, the king, feared his coming and forbade him to enter the city. From afar, the men and women who had gathered outside the town saw him approach. He walked down the road gaily and lightly, vine leaves in his hair, and his skin was brown from the sun. As he walked, he laughed and shouted and the people, seeing his happiness, rushed forward to meet him. They joined him with cheers and song, and soon a multitude marched on the city. Fauns and Bacchantes (ba-kants') bearing cymbals and flutes joined in the procession, and the air was filled with music.

Pentheus the king called his attendants to him. "Go," he commanded, "and seize this vagabond leader of the rabble. Bring him to me! I will soon make him confess that his claim of heavenly parentage is false and make him renounce his false worship!"

His friends and wise counsellors begged him not to oppose the god, but in spite of their pleadings he sent the attendants on their way.

As they approached the throng, the Bacchanals (back'-a-nals) drove them away. In the struggle they captured one and dragged him before the king. Pentheus shook with rage when he beheld the Bacchanal. "Fellow!" he cried. "You shall be put to death! And your fate will be a warning to others. But first, speak, and tell us who you are and what are these new rites you dare to celebrate?"

The prisoner stood before the king and smiled calmly. "My name is Acetes," he said. "My country is Maeonia. My parents were poor people, who had no flocks to leave me. But they left me their fishing rods and nets and the knowledge of their trade. I grew weary of remaining in one place and I learned the pilot's art, and how to guide my course by the stars. One day, I was sailing for Delos, and when we stopped at the island of Dia, I went ashore. The next morning I sent my men for fresh water, and climbed to the top of the highest hill on the island to test the wind. After a time, my men returned bringing with them a young boy whom they had found asleep. He was a delicate-looking child, and they judged he was a noble youth, perhaps a king's son. They hoped to get a liberal ransom for him. I looked at his face, his robes and his walk, and it seemed to me that there was something more than mortal in them. I said to my men, 'What god is concealed in this form, I do not know, but one there certainly is.' Turning to the boy I asked his pardon for the violence done him.

"My men turned on me in rage and pushed the boy toward our ship. I tried to fight them off, but one great strong fellow seized me by the throat and tried to throw me into the sea.

"The young boy seemed to be in a dream, but suddenly he threw off his lethargy and cried out. 'What are you doing to me? What is this fighting for? Who brought me here? Where are you going to carry me?'

"One of the sailors replied, 'Fear nothing. Tell us where you want to go and we will take you there.'

" 'Naxos is my home,' the boy said. 'Take me there and you shall be well rewarded!'

"My crew promised to do so, and ordered me to pilot the ship to Naxos. Now, Naxos lay to the right, and I was trimming the sails to carry us there, when the men of my crew began to signal to me, some by signs and others by muttered threats, to sail in the opposite direction to Egypt, where the boy could be sold as a slave. 'Let someone else pilot the ship,' I said, not wishing to have any part in this wickedness. They cursed me and one of them took my place at the helm and we set sail.

"The boy came to me and confided to me that he was Bacchus, son of Jupiter, and bade me have no fear. Returning to the others, he pretended to weep and said pitifully, 'Sailors, these are not the shores you promised me. Yonder island is not my home. What have I done that you should treat me so?'

"He spoke so sadly that I wept to hear him and the crew laughed at both of us.

"All at once, though you may not believe me, the vessel stopped. She stopped in midsea, as fast as if she were fixed to the ground. The men, struck dumb

193

with astonishment, pulled at their oars and spread more sail, but the ship would not stir. Ivy appeared over her sides and twined around the oars. It crept up to the sails and bore heavy clusters of berries. A vine, laden with grapes, ran up the mast and along the sides of the ship. The sound of flutes was heard and the odor of fragrant wine filled the air. Turning to Bacchus, I saw that he wore a chaplet of vine leaves and bore in his hand a spear wreathed with ivy. Tigers crouched at his feet, and lynxes and spotted panthers played around him as tame as cats.

"The men were seized with terror. Some leapt overboard in madness and when their companions started to follow, they saw that the men in the water were changing shape, their bodies flattening and their legs forming crooked tails. One man cried, 'What miracle is this?' And as he spoke, his mouth widened, his nostrils expanded and scales covered his body. Another terrified soul tried to pull at his oar, and felt his hands shrink up and turn to fins. Still another, trying to raise his arms to a rope, found he had no arms, and curving his mutilated body into an arch, he jumped into the sea. His legs became a crescent-shaped tail. The whole crew were soon in the water, changed into dolphins, and they swam about the

ship, now cutting the surface of the water, now under it, scattering the spray and spouting the water from their broad nostrils. Of twenty men, I alone was left.

"I knelt before Bacchus trembling with fear. 'Fear not,' he said. 'Steer toward Naxos.' I obeyed, and when we arrived there I gladly kindled the altars and celebrated the sacred rites of Bacchus."

When the Bacchanal had finished his story, Pentheus laughed scornfully. "We have wasted enough time listening to these silly lies," he said. "Take him away and kill him without more delay."

The attendants led Acetes away and shut him up in prison. Then, while they were getting ready for the execution, the prison doors opened of their own accord, the chains fell from the prisoner's limbs, and when the attendants looked for him, he was nowhere to be found.

Even this warning did not frighten Pentheus the king, and he decided to go himself to the scene of the wild celebration. The mountain Cithaeron (sih-thee'-ron) was alive with the worshippers of Bacchus and the cries of the Bacchanals could be heard for miles. The noise infuriated Pentheus. He pushed through the wood to an open space where the rites were being held. The women saw him as he came into the clearing, and first among them was his own mother, Agave (a-gay'-veh), blinded by the god. Not recognizing him, she cried out, "See! There is a wild boar, the hugest monster that prowls these woods. Come on, sisters! I will be the first to strike him."

The band rushed upon him, and although he begged for mercy, calling to his mother to save him,

196

they pressed closer to him. Seeing his aunts fighting in the maddened throng he called to them and implored them to protect him from his mother. But they, too, were blinded. Autonoe (o-ton'-o-ee) seized one of his arms and Ino (eye'-no) the other, and while his mother shouted, "Victory! We have won it! The glory is ours!"—he was torn to pieces.

The soft red wine that Bacchus had pressed from the purple grapes became a poison when it was misused. And the people, drunk with it, established the worship of Bacchus in Greece.

CHAPTER XXI

The Punishment of Erysichthon:

ERYSICHTHON (er-ih-sick'-thon) was a rough, loud-mouthed braggart, uncouth in his ways. He boasted that he despised the gods, and defied them to do him harm. One day he was out cutting wood, and after destroying the trees in one section, he entered the sacred grove of Ceres, goddess of Agriculture. A tremendous oak grew in this lovely grove. It was so old and had grown so large that it was almost a wood in itself. Worshippers of Ceres had hung garlands on its boughs, and these garlands were inscribed with messages expressing the gratitude of the givers to the nymph of the tree. At night the Dryades danced around the old oak, hand in hand. Everyone for miles around loved the tree and so many tales were told about it that travelers journeyed miles to see it. It was seventeen feet around and it overtopped the other trees as they overtopped the shrubbery.

Erysichthon's eyes lighted greedily when he saw it. He did not see the beauty of its towering branches or the loveliness of its fresh green leaves. He thought only of the money it would bring him. Calling to his servants, he ordered them to cut it down, and when they refused, he seized his ax and cried out, "What do I care if this is a tree beloved by a goddess? If it were the goddess herself, it would still come down, if it stood in my way."

He lifted his ax, and the oak shuddered and groaned. The servants drew back in terror and begged Erysichthon to spare the tree. But he swung at the oak and the ax dug deep into the bark. Blood spurted from the wound. Nearby villagers, hearing the pitiful groans that issued from the tree, rushed to the spot. When they saw blood gushing to the ground, they drew back horrorstruck. One young man rushed forward and tried to hold back the fatal ax but Erysichthon, maddened and vengeful, cried, "Receive the reward of your piety!" And lifting his ax once more, he struck the young man time and again, inflicting many wounds on his body. Then, he swung again and cut off his head.

As the young man lay on the soft grass which was stained scarlet by his blood, a voice came from within the oak. "I am the nymph who dwells in this tree," it said. "I was beloved by Ceres, and, dying at your hands, Erysichthon, warn you that punishment awaits you."

Erysichthon kicked at the body of the young man with his foot, and started once more for the tree. Blow after blow fell on its bark. Leaves fluttered to the earth, and boughs dropped. He was like a madman and screamed as he struck. Soon the oak trembled and with a mighty crash fell to the ground, carrying most of the trees in the grove with it.

The Dryades were filled with grief at the loss of one of their sisters, and angered at seeing the pride of the forest laid low, went in a body to Ceres. They wore garments of mourning and begged her to punish Erysichthon for his evil deed. She nodded her assent, and as she bowed her head the grain, ripe for harvest in the laden fields, bowed also. She planned a dreadful punishment—to deliver him over to Famine. Ceres herself could not approach Famine, as the Fates had ordained that these two goddesses should never meet, and she called an Oread (oh'-re-ad) from her mountain and said to her, "There is a place in the farthest

part of ice-clad Scythia. It is a sad and sterile region
without trees and without crops. Cold dwells there,
and Fear, and Shuddering, and Famine. Go and tell
Famine to take possession of the bowels of Erysichthon. Tell her not to be subdued by abundance, nor
to let the power of my gifts drive her away. And do
not be alarmed by the distance, but take my chariot.
The dragons are fleet and obey the rein, and will
carry you through the air in a short time."

When she had finished speaking, she handed the

reins to the Oread and gave her her blessing. The young Oread drove away and soon reached Scythia. On arriving at Mount Caucasus, she stopped the dragons and, looking around, saw Famine in a stony field, pulling up the scanty herbage with her teeth and claws. Her hair was rough, her eyes sunk, her face pale, her lips blanched, her jaws covered with dust, and her skin was drawn so tightly that her bones showed and she looked like a skeleton. As the Oread saw her from the distance, for she did not dare come near, she delivered Ceres' message. And, though she stopped as short a time as possible, and kept her distance as well as she could, she had already begun to feel hungry. Hastily, she turned the dragons' heads and drove back to Thessaly.

Famine obeyed the commands of Ceres and sped through the air to the house where Erysichthon lived. She entered his bedchamber and found him asleep. She enfolded him with her wings and breathed herself into him. Then having fulfilled her mission, she hastily left the land of plenty and returned to her accustomed haunts.

Erysichthon still slept, and in his dreams he craved food, and moved his jaws as if in eating. When he awoke his hunger was raging. Without a moment's delay, he called for food, and still complained of hunger even as he ate. Food sufficient for the entire population of a city was set before him, but it was not enough. The more he ate, the more he craved. His hunger was like the sea which receives all the rivers, yet is never filled. It was like the fire that burns all the fuel heaped on it, yet is voracious for more.

His property rapidly diminished under the unceasing demands of his appetite, but his hunger continued unabated. At last, he spent all he had and dismissed all his servants. Only his daughter remained. She was a lovely young girl and worthy of a better parent. *Her, too, he sold!* When she heard what he had done, she ran to the shore, and raised her hands to Neptune in prayer. The man who had bought her followed her, and fearful lest his prize escape, hurried to the beach. But Neptune changed her into a fisherman. Her master, seeing that a fisherman stood in the spot where the maiden had been but a moment before, said suspiciously, "Good fisherman, whither went the maiden whom I saw just now, with hair disheveled and in humble garb, standing about where you stand?"

Rejoicing that her prayer had been answered, she replied, "I have seen nothing, stranger. I have been so intent upon my line that I have noticed nothing else. And I wish I may never catch another fish if I believe any woman or any person except myself to have been hereabouts for some time."

Her master was deceived and went his way, thinking his slave had escaped. Then she assumed her own form. Erysichthon was delighted to find her still with him, and the money that he had got by the sale of her. So he sold her again. This time she was changed by Neptune into a bird, and as often as she was sold, she took on another shape. Sometimes, she was a horse, then an ox, a stag, or a hare. Each time she escaped and ran home. By this base method, her starving father procured the food that he craved.

Still his hunger raged in him, like a consuming fire, and at last, unable to satisfy his passion, he ate his own limbs, and his body, until there was nothing left of him but a huge gaping mouth which Ceres, turning her head away in disgust, destroyed.

CHAPTER XXII

Orpheus, the God of Music:

ORPHEUS (or'-fuse) was the son of Apollo and the Muse Calliope. When he was a little boy, his father gave him a lyre, and he learned to play on it so beautifully that the animals in the forests grew tame and drew near to hear him. Even the trees gathered around him and the rocks softened as the strains of his music filled the air.

In time, he fell in love with a beautiful maiden named Eurydice and married her. Hymen had been invited to the wedding to bless the union, but as he lit their hearthfire with his torch, it smoked badly and brought tears to the eyes of the wedding guests. This was a bad omen, and prophesied trouble for the young couple. For a while, Orpheus and Eurydice (u-rid'-i-see) were very happy. Then, one day, as Eurydice wandered in the fields with her nymphs, she came upon the shepherd Aristaeus (ar-is-tee'-us), who was so struck by her beauty that he seized her arm and drew her to him. She was frightened and turned to run away from him, and, as she turned, she stepped on a venomous snake and was bitten fatally on the foot. She fell to the ground and before Orpheus could reach her, she died.

In despair, Orpheus took his lyre and wandered from land to land, singing his grief to gods and men. Meeting no one who would help him find his lost wife, he resolved to go to the regions of the dead and look for her. He descended into the earth by way of a cave and soon reached the Stygian kingdom. Ghosts crowded about him as he walked and followed him as he presented himself before the thrones of Pluto and Proserpina. Here he drew forth his lyre and began to sing to them. "O deities of the underworld," he sang, "all of us who live must one day come to you. Hear my words, listen to my plea. I did not come here to spy out the secrets of Tartarus, nor to try my strength against the three-headed dog with snaky hair that guards the entrance to your realm. I come to seek my wife who was stung to death by a poisonous viper. Love has led me here. I implore

you to restore Eurydice to me. When she has filled
her term of life, she will gladly return to you. But
give her to me now, I beseech you. If you do not, I
cannot return alone, and you shall triumph in the
death of us both."

As he sang, the ghosts shed tears, and Tantalus, in
spite of his thirst, stopped trying to reach the water
that receded when he stooped to drink it. Ixion's
(icks-eye'-on) wheel stood still, the vulture ceased to
tear the giant's liver, the daughters of Danae rested
from their task of drawing water in a sieve, and Sisy-

phus (sis'-i-fus) sat on his rock to listen. The cheeks of the Furies were wet with tears for the first time. Beautiful Proserpina could not resist the plaintive strains of Orpheus' lyre, and begged her husband Pluto to send for Eurydice.

She came forth from the newly arrived ghosts, limping on her wounded foot. Then Pluto spoke. "You may take your wife away from this sad country," he said to Orpheus, "under one condition. You must not turn round to look at her until you reach the upper air."

Orpheus agreed gladly, and, thanking Pluto, he went toward the gates with Eurydice following a little distance behind him. They walked through passages that were dark and steep, not speaking to each other, and they nearly reached the outlet that led into the cheerful upperworld, when Orpheus, to assure himself that his wife was still following, looked behind. The instant they looked into each other's eyes, she was borne away. Stretching his arms out to embrace her, he grasped only air. Dying now a second time, she felt too tenderly toward her husband to utter a sound of reproach. "Farewell," she cried sadly. "A last farewell."

Her voice was faint, and he could scarcely hear

her. He tried to follow her, and begged permission to return and try once more for her release, but the stern ferryman repulsed him and refused him passage. For seven days he lingered about the brink, refusing food and drink. Then bitterly accusing the powers of Erebus, he sang his sorrow to the rocks and mountains, and his music melted the hearts of the fierce wild tigers and moved the hardy oaks from the earth.

Wandering about the earth, he held himself aloof from all womankind. The Thracian maidens tried their best to captivate him, but he repulsed their advances. Infuriated by his refusal to love them, they planned to kill him. And one day, one of them finding him asleep, threw her javelin at him, crying, "See our despiser! Let him perish." The weapon, hearing the echo of his lyre, fell harmless at his feet. They threw stones at him, and the stones turned aside. Then the enraged women screamed loudly and drowned the voice of the music. The weapons they hurled found their mark, and soon were stained by his blood. The maniacal women tore him limb from limb, and threw his head and lyre into the river Hebrus, down which they floated, murmuring sad music. The trees on the shore bowed their heads in grief and responded with a soft symphony. The Muses gathered up the fragments of his body and buried them in Libethra, where the nightingale still sings sweetly over his grave. His lyre was placed by Jupiter among the stars.

His soul, freed from the body that bound it to earth, wandered once more to Tartarus, where he found his Eurydice. They roam the happy fields together now, and Orpheus gazes into her eyes as often as he wishes, no longer fearful of losing her for a thoughtless glance.

CHAPTER XXIII

Pyramus and Thisbe:

IN BABYLON, where Semiramis (se-mir'-a-mis) reigned as queen, there lived a youth named Pyramus (pir'-a-mus) and a maiden named Thisbe (thiz'-be). He was the handsomest young man in all the land, while she was the most beautiful girl. Their parents occupied adjoining houses, and as children the two had been constant companions. As they grew older, it was almost inevitable that their childish friendship should turn into love. Confronting their parents, they told them that they wished to marry, but the two families, for some reason, opposed the match. And Pyramus and Thisbe were forbidden to see, or even to speak to each other.

This was more than they could bear, and while they did not speak, they conversed by signs and glances. Their love burned stronger and stronger every day, until, one day, they discovered that the wall that divided the two houses had a small crack in it. Overjoyed by this discovery, they forgot what their parents had said, and whispered messages of love and encouragement through the tiny slit.

As they stood, Pyramus on one side of the wall and Thisbe on the other, their breaths would mingle. "Cruel wall," they murmured softly, "why do you keep two lovers apart? But we will not be ungrateful. We owe you, we confess, the privilege of transmitting loving words to willing ears."

All day, they stood at the wall, whispering together, and when night came and they said goodbye, they pressed their lips to the stone.

Next morning, when Aurora, goddess of the dawn, had put out the stars and the sun had melted the frost from the grass, they met at the wall again. Rebelling against the cruelty of their parents, they decided they would slip away from their homes that very night and walk beyond the city's bounds, where they would meet at the Tomb of Ninus (nigh'-nus). The one who came first should await the other at the foot of a white mulberry tree that stood near a cool spring.

All day long, they waited impatiently for the sun to go down beneath the waters and the night to rise up from them. When it was dark, Thisbe crept out of the house, her head covered with a veil, and stealthily making her way to the Tomb, she sat down under the mulberry tree to wait for Pyramus. As she sat alone, she saw a huge lioness, her jaws dripping with blood from a recent slaughter, approach the spring to drink. Thisbe fled in terror and hid in the hollow of a rock. As she ran, she dropped her veil, and the lioness, seeing the veil on the ground, tossed and tore it with her bloody mouth.

It was some time before Pyramus could leave his house without being observed, and when he arrived at the appointed meeting place, he was out of breath. There was no sign of Thisbe. In the sand, he saw the footprints of the lioness and he grew pale with fright. He followed the prints and came upon Thisbe's veil, torn and bloody. "O hapless girl!" he cried in agony. "I have been the cause of thy death! Thou, more worthy of life than I, hast fallen first victim. I will follow. I am the guilty cause in tempting thee forth to a place of such peril, and not being myself on the spot to guard thee. Come forth, ye lions, from the rocks, and tear this guilty body with your teeth!" He picked up the veil from the ground and carried it to a spot beneath the white mulberry tree, covering it with tears and kisses. For a while he lay there sobbing, then drawing his sword, he said, "My blood also shall stain your texture."

He plunged the sword into his heart. The blood spurted from the wound and tinged the white mulberries of the tree a dark red. It even sank into earth and the red color mounted through the trunk to the fruit.

Thisbe, hidden in the hollow of the rock, still shook with terror, but not wishing to keep her lover waiting too long, she ventured forth and crept cautiously out. When she came to the spot where Pyramus was to meet her, she saw the changed color of the berries and doubted whether it was the same place. As she hesitated, she saw someone struggling on the ground in the throes of death. Thinking the lioness had claimed another victim, she started to run away. Just then the moon appeared from behind a cloud and she recognized Pyramus dying at her feet.

She screamed and beat her breast. "O Pyramus," she cried. "What has done this? Answer me, Pyramus. It is your own Thisbe who speaks. Hear me, dearest, and lift your drooping head."

Pyramus opened his eyes and closed them again. Shuddering, he died.

Thisbe threw herself on his lifeless body. By his side she saw the empty scabbard of his sword and, beneath it, her veil, torn and stained with blood.

She kissed him gently. "Thine own hand has slayed thee, and for my sake," she whispered softly. "I, too, can be brave for once, and my love is as strong as thine. I will follow thee in death, for I have been the cause. And death, which alone could part us, shall not prevent my joining thee. And ye, unhappy parents of us both, deny us not our united request. As love and death joined us, let one tomb contain us. And thou, tree, retain the marks of our slaughter. Let thy berries still serve for memorials of our blood."

She arose, and after a last look at Pyramus, plunged the sword into her breast.

When the distracted parents found the bodies of the beautiful maiden and the handsome youth, they were filled with remorse. They appealed to the gods, and the gods told them of Thisbe's dying wish. The two lovers were buried side by side in one sepulchre, and the mulberry tree, forever after, brought forth dark red berries.

CHAPTER XXIV

The Trojan War:

WHEN Peleus, one of the heroes of the Argonautic Expedition, was married to Thetis (thee'-tis), the loveliest of the Nereides, all the gods and goddesses were invited to the wedding feast with the exception of Eris (ee'-ris), goddess of Discord. Enraged at the slight, she threw a golden apple among the guests, which bore the inscription: "For the fairest."

Juno, Venus and Minerva each claimed the apple, and soon were quarreling bitterly. Jupiter was not willing to decide in so delicate a matter, and he sent the goddesses to Mount Ida, where the beautiful shepherd Paris, the son of Priam, King of Troy, was tending his flocks. He asked Paris to make the decision. The goddesses gathered around him, extolling their own charms, and each one promised to reward him if he gave her the prize. Juno promised him power and riches; Minerva told him that she would see that he gained glory and renown; and Venus whispered that he should have the fairest woman in the world for his wife. Paris decided in favor of Venus and gave her the golden apple, thus making the two other goddesses his enemies.

Under the protection of Venus, Paris sailed for Greece, where he was hospitably received by Menelaus (men-e-lay'-us), king of Sparta. Now Helena, the wife of Menelaus, was the very woman whom Venus had destined for Paris. She was the most beautiful woman in the world, and had been sought as a bride by hundreds of suitors. The young men loved her so devotedly that they swore that no matter which of them she chose to wed, the others would defend her from harm all her life. She married Menelaus and was living with him happily when Paris became their guest.

Paris, aided by Venus, persuaded her to elope with him, and carried her to Troy. Overcome by grief, Menelaus called upon his brother chieftains of Greece to fulfill their pledges and join him in his efforts to recover his wife. Only one of them held back. His name was Ulysses, and he had married a woman named Penelope (peh-nel'-o-peh) and was happy with his wife and child. He had no wish to embark on such a troublesome affair. Palamedes (pal-a-mee′-deez), one of his friends, was sent to beg him to join the quest, and when he arrived at Ithaca where Ulysses lived, Ulysses pretended to be mad. Seeing Palamedes approaching, he hastily yoked an ass and an ox together to the plough and began to sow salt. Palamedes, suspecting a ruse, placed Ulysses' child before the plough, whereupon the father turned the plough aside, showing plainly that he was no madman. After that, he could no longer refuse to fulfill his promise.

Now, although Paris was the son of Priam, king of Troy, he had been brought up in obscurity, as the oracle had prophesied that he would one day be the ruin of the state. And with his entrance into Troy with Helena, these forebodings seemed likely to be realized. The army which was being assembled in Greece was the greatest that had ever been known. Agamemnon (ag-a-mem′-non), brother of Menelaus, was chosen as commander-in-chief. Achilles (a-kill′-eez) was their most illustrious warrior. After him, ranked Ajax, who was gigantic in size and had great courage, though he was dull in intellect. Diomedes (dy-o-mee′deez) was enlisted, a man who had all the qualities of a hero. There was Ulysses, famous for his sagacity, and Nestor, the oldest of the Grecian chiefs.

Troy was no feeble enemy. Priam the king was now an old man, but he had been a wise ruler and had strengthened his state by good government at home and numerous alliances with his neighbors. The principal stay and support of his throne was his son Hector. He was a brave, noble young man, and he felt a presentiment of danger, when he realized the great wrong his brother Paris had done in bringing Helena back to Troy. He knew that he must fight for his family and country, yet he was sick with grief at the foolish circumstances that had set hero against hero. He was married to Andromache (an-drom'-a-keh). The principal leaders on the side of the Trojans were, besides Hector, Aeneas (e-nee'-as), Deiphobus (de-if'-o-bus), Glaucus (glo'-kus), and Sarpedon (sar-pee'-don).

After two years of preparation, the Greek fleet and army assembled in the port of Aulis (o'-lis). Here they suffered more delays; pestilence broke out in the camps, and there was no wind to fill their sails. Eventually, they set out for the coast of Troy, and plunged at once into a battle with the Trojans. For nine years they fought, neither side winning over the other. The Greeks began to despair of ever conquering the city, and decided to resort to a trick. They pretended to be making ready to abandon the siege, and most of the ships set sail with many warriors on board. They did not head for home, but sailed to a nearby island where they hid in the friendly harbor. The Greeks who were left in the camp built a huge horse of wood, which they said was to be a peace offering to Minerva. They filled it with armed men, instead, and left it in their camp. The remaining Greeks then sailed away.

When the Trojans saw that the encampment had broken up and the fleet had gone, they threw open the gates to the city, and everyone rushed forth to look at the abandoned camp grounds. They found the immense horse and wondered what it could be. Some thought it should be carried back to the city and put on exhibition as a trophy of the war, but others, more cautious, were afraid of it. Laocoon, the priest of Neptune, tried to warn them against it. "What madness, citizens, is this?" he exclaimed. "Have you not learned enough of Grecian fraud to be on your guard against it? For my part, I fear the Greeks even when they offer gifts."

As he spoke, he threw his lance at the horse's side.

It struck, and a hollow sound like a groan came forth from it. The people were almost ready to take his advice and destroy the horse, when a group appeared dragging a young man with them. He appeared to be a Greek prisoner, and he was brought before the Trojan chiefs. They promised him that they would spare his life on one condition; he was to answer truly the questions they asked him.

He told them that he was a Greek named Sinon (sigh'-non), and that he had been abandoned by his countrymen, betrayed by Ulysses, for a trifling offense. He assured them that the wooden horse had been made as an offering to Minerva, and that the Greeks had made it so huge to prevent its being carried into the city. Sinon added that the Greeks had been told that if the Trojans took possession of the horse, the Greeks would lose the war.

Then the people began to think of how they could move the enormous horse into the city. And, suddenly, they saw two immense serpents advancing from the sea. They crawled up on the shore, and the crowd fled in all directions. The serpents slithered to the spot where Laocoon stood with his two sons. First they attacked the children, crushing their bodies and breathing their pestilential breath into the boys'

faces. Laocoon tried to drag his children away, and the serpents wound their bodies around his. He struggled pitifully to free himself, but they soon strangled him and his two sons. In awe, the people crept back to the camp. Talking among themselves, they decided that the gods had taken revenge on Laocoon for talking against the wooden horse, which was a sacred object. And they began to move it into the city in triumph. All day, the Trojans feasted and sang around the horse which they had placed in the main square of Troy. At last, exhausted from the festivities, they went to their homes and fell into their beds.

When the city was quiet, the armed men who were hidden in the body of the horse, were let out by Sinon. They stole to the gates of the city which were closed for the night, and let in their friends who had returned under the cover of darkness. They set fire to the city, and the people, overcome with feasting and sleep, were ruthlessly killed. Troy had fallen.

King Priam was the last to be slain, and he fought bravely to the end.

Menelaus hastened to the palace and found his wife, Helena. And not even the powers of Venus could save Paris from the wrath of his enemies. He was killed, and Menelaus carried his wife safely back to Sparta.

CHAPTER XXV

The Voyage of Ulysses:

WHEN Troy had fallen, Ulysses with his men set sail for home. No sooner were they out of the harbor when a dreadful storm blew up and drove their ship from its course. For nine days they were hopelessly lost at sea, and finally they sighted a small island. It was the country of the Lotus-eaters. Almost dying of thirst, the men first set out to look for water, and when they had refreshed themselves, Ulysses told them to explore the island and find out who the inhabitants were. They set out and soon came upon a group of people who received them hospitably, and offered them some of their own food, the lotus plant, to eat.

Now, when anyone ate a lotus leaf, he immediately forgot all about his home and his family and wanted to remain forever on the island. The men from the ship, half-starved and flattered by the attentions shown them by the islanders, were only too happy to sit down at the table and eat. Ulysses waited a while for his soldiers and then went in search of them. He saw them feasting, and saw what they were eating. Knowing what effect the sweet-tasting drug would have on them, he begged them to come with him. But the men, who were by this time in dreamy half-sleep, did not even hear him. By force, he dragged them away, and even had to tie them to the benches of the ship, until he had hoisted the sails and got under way. The sea air soon cleared their heads and they sailed on.

After many days they sighted the country of the Cyclopes (sigh-klo'-peez). These people were huge giants who had but one eye which was placed in the middle of the forehead. They lived in caves and tended their flocks, eating whatever roots and wild grasses grew on the rocky shores. Ulysses left the main body of his ships at anchor and went with one vessel to the Cyclopes' island to search for supplies. He and his companions landed, and carried with them a jar of wine for a present. They wandered about until they came to a large cave which they entered, and, finding no one about, they set about exploring it. They found it stored with quantities of cheese, pails of milk, lambs and kids in wooden pens, and dried and salted meat. They ate some of the cheese and drank a few pails of milk, and were about to cook a roast of meat, when they heard dreadful noises outside of the cave. Peering out they saw a frightful giant called Polyphemus (pol-i-fee'-mus). He carried an immense bundle of firewood which he threw to the ground at the mouth of the cave. Then he drove his flock of sheep and goats into the cavern to be milked, and when they were safely in, he moved a large stone, closing the entrance. It was so large a stone that twenty oxen could not move it.

As the men quaked with terror, he sat down and milked his ewes. When he had finished, he turned his great eye around and saw the men who huddled in the shadows of the pens. He spoke to them, and his voice was a dreadful growl that echoed from the dripping walls. "Who are you?" he asked. "And where do you come from?"

Ulysses stepped forward and answered him humbly. "We are Greeks," he said, "returning from a great expedition. We have lately won much glory in the conquest of Troy. We are now on our way home, but are lost. And, if you will offer us your hospitality, in the name of the gods, we will restock our larders, and be on our way."

Polyphemus did not answer. He reached out his

great hand and seized two of the Greeks as easily as a man picks a handful of grass. He hurled them against the side of the cave, and dashed out their brains. As their companions stood watching in horror, he pulled the dying men apart and ate them up, clothes and all, not even leaving their bones. Then having made a hearty meal, he stretched himself out on the floor and went to sleep.

Ulysses drew forth his sword, and was about to kill the giant as he slept, when he remembered the huge rock that blocked the entrance to the cave. He realized that if he killed the giant, he and the rest of his men would be hopelessly imprisoned and would eventually die of starvation. All night, the men huddled in fright in the dark, damp cave. They were unable to decide what to do, and when morning came, they were sunk in hopeless despair. The giant awoke and lazily stretched out his hand and grabbed two more of the men. He hurled them against the walls, and feasted on their flesh until there wasn't a fragment left. Then he moved the rock away from the entrance, drove out his flocks, and replaced the barrier after him.

When he was gone, the men came out from their hiding places, and Ulysses tried desperately to plan

how he might avenge the death of his companions, and make his escape with his friends. Searching the cave for a weapon, he came upon a massive bar of wood which had been cut by the Cyclops for a staff. He ordered his men to sharpen the end of it to a fine point and when that was done, they seasoned it in the fire, and hid it under the straw on the floor. Then four of the boldest were selected, and Ulysses told them of his scheme.

It was almost evening when they had finished their tasks, and they soon heard the Cyclops approaching. He rolled away the stone and drove his flock in as usual. After milking them, he seized two more of Ulysses' men, dashed their brains out, and made his evening meal. After he had supped to his content, Ulysses approached him and handed him a bowl of wine, saying, "Cyclops, this is wine. Taste it and drink after eating thy meal of man's flesh."

The giant took it and drank it. He was delighted with the taste of it, and called for more. Ulysses gave him bowl after bowl of the heady drink, and this pleased the giant so much that he promised Ulysses that he should be the last of his party to be devoured. He asked his name, and Ulysses replied, "My name is Noman."

When he had drunk the last of the wine, the giant lay down to sleep. Then Ulysses called to his four friends and, lifting the staff, they thrust the end of it into the fire until it was a burning coal. When it was red hot, they plunged it into the Cyclops' one eye.

The monster roared in pain, and Ulysses and his men sprang back and hid themselves in the cave. Polyphemus bellowed and called out to the other Cyclopes to help him. Hearing his cries, they came from their caves and flocked around his den. "What hurt," they asked, "has caused you to sound an alarm?"

"O friends, I die," he answered, "and Noman gives the blow."

"If Noman gives the blow," they said, "then thou hast been killed by a blow from Jupiter and thou must bear it."

They turned away from the cave, leaving him groaning on the ground. He was not yet dead, and in the morning, he rolled the huge stone aside, and let his flocks out to pasture. Although he couldn't see, he stood at the entrance of the cave to feel of everything that passed him, so that Ulysses and his men should not escape. Ulysses told his companions to harness the rams of the flock three abreast with willow branches which they found on the floor of the cave. To the middle ram of the three, one of the Greeks hung, protected on either side by the other two rams. One by one, the men swung themselves from the shaggy coats of the rams. As they passed the giant, he felt of the animals' backs and sides, but he never thought to feel of their bellies. So all the men escaped, Ulysses being the last one who passed.

Once outside the cavern, the men released themselves and tore to the ship, driving the cattle before them. They hastened aboard and pushed off from shore. When they were a safe distance, Ulysses shouted out, "Cyclops, the gods have repaid thee for thy atrocious deeds! It is Ulysses to whom thou owest thy loss of sight."

The Cyclops, hearing this, bellowed in rage, and seizing a huge rock from the side of the mountain, he hurled it with all his might in the direction of the ship. Down it came, just clearing the vessel's stern. The ocean heaved and threw the ship once more toward the land, and it barely escaped from being dashed against the shore. They pulled away with the utmost difficulty, and Ulysses was about to call to the giant again, but his friends begged him not to do so. He waited until they were far out, and then, unable to resist taunting the Cyclops, he called out again. The giant answered them with curses, but they pulled at their oars, and soon reached the rest of the fleet, and set sail once more.

CHAPTER XXVI

Circe, the Enchantress:

Near the island of the Cyclopes, lay the island of Aeolus (ee'-o-lus). Aeolus ruled the winds, and he sent them forth to fill the sails of ships or kept them chained as he chose. Ulysses and his men landed at the beautiful little island and Aeolus greeted them in a friendly manner. When they were ready to leave, he gave them a leather bag tied with a silver string, which held all the winds that might be harmful or dangerous. He warned Ulysses not to open the bag until he had reached home, and promised that he would, until that time, send forth only his pleasantest breezes.

For nine days the ships of Ulysses sped before the swift breezes of Aeolus, and all that time, Ulysses stood at the wheel, without sleep. At last, exhausted, he lay down to rest. While he slept, the crew approached him and, seeing the leather bag lying by his side, wondered what it could contain. They decided that it must hold some rare treasure which the hospitable king Aeolus had given their commander. They loosed the string and the winds rushed forth with a dreadful sound. The ships were driven from their course again, and back to the island they had left. Here Aeolus, indignant at the folly of the sailors, refused to help them again, and they were obliged to row away from the island.

For weeks they sailed the seas until they came to the Aeaean (ee-ee'-an) isle where Circe, the daughter of the sun, dwelt. Landing on the sloping beach, Ulysses climbed a high hill, and gazing about, saw no signs of habitation except in one spot on the center of the island. There he saw a palace, surrounded by lovely trees.

He ordered one half of his crew under the leadership of Eurylochus to go to the palace and ask for hospitality. The men set forth, and as they approached the palace, they found themselves surrounded by wild beasts—lions, tigers, and wolves. These animals were not at all fierce, and the men looked at them in wonder. Now these animals had once been men, and had been changed by Circe's enchantments into the forms of beasts.

The men drew near the palace, and soon they heard soft music, and a sweet woman's voice singing. Eurylochus called aloud, and the goddess herself came forth and invited them in. The men gladly followed her, all, that is, but Eurylochus who suspected danger. He hid himself in a tall tree where he could look over the hedges and see what befell his men.

The goddess led them to a banquet table and served them with wine and other delicacies. When they had feasted heartily and were more than drunk on the wine and stuffed like pigs with rare food, she touched them with her wand and changed them into swine. Their bodies only were changed, and they retained their human minds. Then she shut them up in sties and supplied them with acorns and other things that swine love.

Eurylochus climbed down from the tree and hurried back to the ship where he told his tale to Ulysses. Ulysses, angered by the loss of his men, determined to go himself, and see if he could find any means to set his companions free. He went alone and as he walked, he met a youth who addressed him familiarly and who seemed to know all about him and his adventures. He told Ulysses that he was Mercury, and warned him of the arts of Circe and of the danger in approaching the palace. Ulysses would not heed the warning, and Mercury gave him a sprig of the plant Moly which was imbued with the power to resist sorceries. He advised Ulysses what he must do, and how best to resist the charms of the lovely goddess.

Ulysses thanked him and went on his way. When he reached the palace, he was received by Circe who entertained him as she had done his companions. And after he had eaten and drunk, she touched him with her wand, saying, "Hereafter, seek the sty and wallow with thy friends."

Instead of obeying, he drew his sword and rushed at her, his face black with fury. She fell to her knees and begged for mercy, and he told her that he would spare her if she swore to release his companions and practise no further arts against them. She led him to the pens and changed the swine back to humans once more. Ulysses was so grateful to her, that he accepted her invitation to stay on the island for a while and rest from their tiresome voyage, and he would have forgotten his native land entirely, had not his companions reminded him of his duty. Circe saw them sadly to their ships, and instructed them how to pass safely by the Sirens.

The Sirens were sea-nymphs who charmed unhappy mariners by their songs, until travelers were irresistibly compelled to throw themselves into the sea. Circe told Ulysses to fill the ears of his seamen with wax so that they could not hear the music, and to have himself bound to the mast with stout ropes. "Warn your men," she said, "that no matter how you plead to be released, they must remain firm, and must not release you until you have passed the Siren's island.

It was well that Ulysses followed her advice, for when they reached the island, the sea was calm, and over the waters came the notes of music so lovely that Ulysses struggled to get loose, and cried to be set free. The men, obedient to his first orders, bound him still tighter, and held to the course. The music grew fainter and fainter, and soon faded in the distance.

CHAPTER XXVII

The Perils of Ulysses:

IN A cave, high up on a rocky cliff, near a narrow passage through which Ulysses's ships had to pass, lived Scylla who had once been a beautiful maiden. When she was still a lovely water nymph, she had spurned the love of Glaucus, a sea deity and a favorite of Circe, and the goddess to punish her had changed her into a monster. Serpents and barking monsters surrounded her, and, more horrible, they were a part of her and she could not drive them away. In shame, she turned from the green waters of the sea she loved and hid herself on the lonely rock. As the years passed, she grew into a beast at heart, and preyed on the mariners who sailed too near her. She had six heads and from every vessel that passed, she seized six of the crew and devoured them. Near the cave where she dwelt, was a gulf named Charybdis (ka-rib'-dis). It was nearly level with the water, but

three times each day the water rushed into it with terrific force, and three times the tide rushed back. Any ship coming near the whirlpool when the tide was rushing in, was carried down to the blackest depths of the ocean, and not even Neptune could save it.

Circe had warned Ulysses of these two dangers, and as they approached the dreadful places, he kept strict watch to discover them. The roar of waters from Charybdis could be heard from a distance, but Scylla could not be seen. While Ulysses and his men watched the dreadful whirlpool with anxious eyes, they were not on guard from the attack from Scylla, who darted her snaky heads down and caught six of his men from the deck of the ship and bore them away shrieking to her den. It was the saddest sight Ulysses had yet seen as he felt powerless to save them. Soon their cries were stilled, and Scylla, sated with human blood, allowed the ship to pass.

After passing Scylla and Charybdis, Ulysses' ships came in sight of the land of Thrinacia. On this island the cattle of Hyperion were pastured, tended by his daughters, Lampetia and Phaethusa. Circe had warned Ulysses that these flocks must not be molested, no matter what the wants of the voyagers might be. She cautioned him that if her warning was not heeded, and the flocks were touched, destruction was sure to fall on the entire crew.

Ulysses would gladly have passed the island without stopping, but his companions begged for rest and refreshment, and Ulysses yielded. He made them swear that they would not touch one animal of the sacred flocks and herds, and would be content with the provisions they had left on board the ships. They landed, and as long as the provisions lasted, the men kept their oath, but when their food was gone, they were forced to rely on what birds and fishes they could catch near the shores. Driven reckless by hunger, they killed some of the cattle, and tried to make amends for their deed by offering a portion of the kill to the gods. Ulysses had been overseeing some repairs to his ships when the cattle were slain, and when he returned to land, he was horrified at what his men had done. The men were already preparing the meat to eat, and Ulysses, looking down at the skins of the animals, saw the hides creep along the ground, and heard the joints of meat lowing plaintively as they turned on the spit.

He bade his men make haste to set sail, and they

hurried away from the island, thinking that they had escaped punishment. No sooner were they at sea than the fair weather changed. A storm blew up. A stroke of lightning shattered their mast, and killed the pilot. At last the vessel, beaten by the waves, fell to pieces. The keel and the mast floated side by side and Ulysses made them into a raft to which he clung. The rest of the crew perished in the waves. Through the dark night Ulysses held to the raft, and by morning he had drifted to Calypso's (ka-lip'-so) island.

Calypso was a sea-nymph, and she saw Ulysses on the raft just as he was about to be dashed to death on the rocks. She pulled him from the sea and brought him food and drink. For many days he lay in her grotto near death while she nursed him back to health. She made him a bed of fragrant violets, and would have kept him with her, had not Jupiter bade her to send Ulysses on his way. Together they built a sturdy new raft, and provisioned it well. Calypso sadly saw him sail out to sea. He journeyed for many days and, in sight of land, another storm broke out. His mast fell and great cracks appeared beneath his feet. Calypso, learning of his plight, sent a sea-nymph to him who took the form of a cormorant and lighted on his sinking raft. She gave him a girdle and told him to bind it beneath his breast, and it would buoy him up as he swam to land.

Ulysses clung to the raft until it fell apart. Then, plunging into the sea, he began to swim. Minerva smoothed the waves before him and sent him a wind that carried him toward shore. The surf beat high on the rocks, but he soon found calmer water at the mouth of a gentle stream where he landed, breathless and nearly dead. He kissed the soil, and lay down to sleep.

CHAPTER XXVIII

The End of Ulysses' Voyage:

THE land where Ulysses had fallen exhausted was Scheria, the country of the Phaeacians. These people had originally dwelt near the Cyclopes, but after many quarrels with that savage race, they migrated to another island. They were a peaceful, godlike people, and the gods themselves often appeared among them. Their island was so remote from the wars of the mainland that the Phaeacians no longer made weapons, and almost forgot the use of the bow and arrow.

On the night Ulysses swam ashore, and while he lay sleeping on his bed of leaves, the daughter of the king of the island had a dream. She dreamed that Minerva appeared before her to remind her that her wedding day was not far distant, and that it would be wise to wash all the family clothes for the great occasion. This was quite a task, as the fountains were far away, and all the garments had to be carried to them. When the princess awoke, she told her parents about her dream, not alluding to her wedding day, but substituting another reason just as good. Her father ordered grooms to harness a wagon into which the clothes were piled, and her mother, the queen, packed her a lunch of food and wine. The princess climbed into the cart, while her lovely attendants followed on foot. They arrived at the riverside, turned the mules out to graze, and unloaded the wagon. They worked with speed and cheerfulness, and it was no time at all until the clothes were clean and spread on the shore to dry. They bathed themselves and sat down beneath a tree for a picnic lunch. When they had eaten, they amused themselves with a game of ball, and Minerva, who had been watching them, caused the ball thrown by the princess to fall into the water. At that they all screamed and the noise awoke Ulysses.

He looked through the bushes and saw a group of maidens. By their dress and actions, he knew they were of high rank. He needed help sadly, but how could he venture forth naked and ask them to aid him? Breaking off a leafy branch from a tree, he held it before him and stepped out from the thicket. The young girls screamed again when they saw him and fled in all directions—all but Nausicaa, the princess.

Ulysses told her his story and begged her for food and clothing. The princess promised him her father's hospitality, and called back her attendants, scolding them for their foolish fears. "This man," she said, "is an unhappy wanderer. It is our duty to cherish him. Phaeacians have no enemies to fear, and the poor and needy are sent to us by Jupiter. Go bring him food and clothing from the wagon. You will find my brother's garments there, washed clean and fresh."

Ulysses bathed, and put on the clothes the maidens brought him. When the princess saw him clad in the splendid robes, she whispered to her maidens that she wished the gods would send her such a husband, and, turning to Ulysses, she asked him to follow them to the city. "But when we draw near it," she added, "wait in a grove, for I fear the remarks that might be made by the people if they see me return with a gallant stranger."

He agreed to hide in the grove, and follow her to

the palace later. After allowing her time to reach the palace, he went his way, and as he neared the outskirts of the city, he met a young woman who was carrying a pitcher to the well. It was Minerva who had assumed this form. Ulysses asked her to direct him to the palace of the king, and the maiden offered to be his guide. Under the guidance of the goddess and by her power enveloped in a cloud that shielded him from sight, Ulysses passed among the busy crowd and looked with wonder at their harbor, their ships, their forum, and their battlements, until he came to the palace. Here the goddess left him.

Ulysses, before entering the courtyard of the palace, stood and gazed about him. The splendor of the scene astonished him. Bronze walls stretched from the entrance to the interior house. The doors were gold. The doorposts were carved out of silver, and the lintels were silver ornamented with gold. Along the walls were seats covered with scarves of the finest texture, the work of the Phaeacian maidens, and on these seats the princes sat and feasted, while golden statues of graceful youths held lighted torches in their hands which shed a soft radiance over everything. Fifty women served in the household. Some were employed to grind the corn, others to wind off the purple wool or ply the loom. For the Phaeacian women as far exceeded all other women in household arts as the mariners of their country did the rest of mankind in the management of ships.

A spacious garden lay outside the court, filled with pear, pomegranate, apple, fig and olive trees. Neither winter's cold nor summer's drought arrested their growth, and they flourished in constant succession, some budding while others were maturing. In one part of the garden one could see the vines, some in blossom, some loaded with grapes. On the garden's borders, flowers bloomed all year, and the air was sweet with their perfume. In the center of the garden two fountains poured forth their waters.

Ulysses was filled with admiration. He was not observed by the others as he was still enveloped in the cloud Minerva had thrown around him. After feasting his eyes on all the beauty he went into the hall where the chiefs and senators were assembled. They were pouring a libation to Mercury, whose worship followed the evening meal. Just then, Minerva dissolved the cloud that surrounded Ulysses. He walked to the queen's throne, knelt at her feet, and implored her favor and assistance to enable him to return to his native country. Then, withdrawing, he seated himself in the manner of suppliants, by the hearthside.

For a time, no one spoke. At last an aged statesman, addressing the king, said, "It is not fit that a stranger who asks our hospitality should be kept waiting in supplicant guise. Let him therefore be led to a seat and supplied with food and wine."

The king arose, took Ulysses by the hand, and led him to the table. He dismissed his guests, and Ulysses was left alone with the king and queen. The queen, recognizing the clothes he wore as those which her maidens and herself had made, asked him from whom he had received these garments. He told them of the wreck of his raft, his escape by swimming, and the help given him by the princess. The royal couple heard his story, and promised to furnish him with a ship so that he might return to his native land.

The next day, a bark was prepared and a crew of stout rowers selected. Then everyone went to the palace where a great banquet had been prepared. After the feast, the young men of the country showed Ulysses their skill in running and wrestling, and challenged him to show what he could do. He arose from his seat and seized a quoit far heavier than any the Phaeacians had thrown, and sent it farther than the utmost throw of theirs.

After the games, they returned to the hall and the herald led in Demodocus, the blind bard. He took for his theme the story of the Wooden Horse. Apollo inspired him and he sang so feelingly of the terrors and exploits of that eventful time that Ulysses was moved to tears. When the king saw his grief, he turned to him. "Why are your sorrows awakened at the mention of Troy?" he asked. "Did you lose a father or brother there? Or perhaps a dear friend?"

Ulysses told him that he himself had fought at Troy, and recounted all the adventures which had befallen him since his departure from that city. The king was so moved at his tale that he proposed that all the chiefs should present Ulysses with a gift. They obeyed, and vied with one another in loading the illustrious stranger with costly things.

The next day Ulysses set sail, and in a short time arrived at Ithaca, his own island. When the vessel touched the strand, he was asleep, and the mariners, without awaking him, carried him ashore. They laid him on the chest which contained his presents, and then sailed away.

Ulysses was safe at home, at last. But Neptune

was so angry with the Phaeacians for rescuing Ulysses from his hands that on the return of the Phaeacian ship into its own port he transformed it into a rock, opposite the mouth of the harbor.